TORCHED

Summer of '64

JOE EDD MORRIS

Black Rose Writing | Texas

The author grants the final approval for this literary material.

First printing

This is a work of fiction. Names, characters, businesses, places, events, and incidents are either the products of the author's imagination or used in a fictitious manner. Any resemblance to actual persons, living or dead, or actual events is purely coincidental.

ISBN: 978-1-68433-474-2
PUBLISHED BY BLACK ROSE WRITING
www.blackrosewriting.com

Printed in the United States of America
Suggested Retail Price (SRP) $17.95

Torched: Summer of '64 is printed in Baskerville

*As a planet-friendly publisher, Black Rose Writing does its best to eliminate unnecessary waste to reduce paper usage and energy costs, while never compromising the reading experience. As a result, the final word count vs. page count may not meet common expectations.

To Michael Hartnett, a brother in every way but blood.

In memory of all those who, during that summer, made the ultimate sacrifice and gave their lives for freedom.

"Greater love has no man than this, that he lay down his life for his friends."
—Gospel of John 15:13

"For the white volunteers it was the Freedom Summer; for black Americans, in Mississippi and elsewhere, almost two decades later it is still The Summer That Didn't End."
—Julian Bond, November 1991

PRAISE FOR
JOE EDD MORRIS'S *THE PRISON*

"Fast-paced storyline with several twists and possible plot directions throughout keep the reader guessing... difficult to put down." *–BookZilla*

"A Brilliant Novel!" –Michael Hartnett, author of *Generation Dementia*

"A stunning achievement by an accomplished writer of remarkable talent." –Jim Hutchingson, co-author of *Boundaries*

AUTHOR'S NOTE

New Albany and Holmes County, Mississippi, are real places. Most of the events from the Civil Rights Movement and Freedom Summer of '64 actually occurred. In honor of their time and lives, I have retained many of the actual names. But this is a work of fiction and all other names and characters are fictional. Any resemblance to persons living or dead is purely coincidental. Except for Giles Word, Lula Peterson and David Wade. They were flesh and blood.

TORCHED

Summer of '64

PART 1

PART I

1

The sign said ENTERING HOLMES COUNTY and another a few miles down the road, MOUNT PLEASANT, MISS. POPULATION 201.

I had driven from Atlanta, unaware that more than one thousand volunteers following training seminars at Oxford, Ohio, were also headed to Mississippi for their Summer Project. I drove unaware that a black Methodist church in nearby Neshoba County would be burned three nights later by nightriders. I drove unaware that, fifteen days later, James Chaney, Michael Schwerner and Andy Goodman would be missing. I drove completely and totally unaware that I was headed toward a summer that would forever be remembered as "the mother of all summers" and that I'd be smack in the middle of it.

I passed a service station, then a cotton gin and stopped at a traffic light. The main street was a row of storefronts—a bank, a hardware store, several retail stores and a post office. They were old structures, set back and elevated above street level creating the appearance of a Hollywood stage set. Hitching-posts would have easily placed the scene before the turn of the century.

Mrs. Stowes, my seminary intern director, had said the highway might not be marked, and she was right. From the map she gave to me, I knew to take a right at the traffic light onto State 440. In this one horse town, I sat through a long light that should've been in Atlanta at Peachtree and Wall. While waiting, I saw a poster on a nearby utility pole.

The face was Uncle Sam's. I'd seen a similar poster as a child and recalled the man I was with when I saw it and the questions it evoked.

*   *   *

"Uncle Giles, were you ever a soldier?"

He nodded a couple of times.

"Uncle Giles, did you ever kill a man?"

His head stopped nodding. He looked away, sighed heavily, and with sweat glistening on his large black face, locked eyes with me.

"'Fraid so, Chile. 'Fraid so. Not somethin' a man likes to talk about."

Then he told me, gently and seriously, about a bloody battle on a freezing and snowy December day. About the surprise attack and the heroic stand of the 106th Infantry Division that stalled the Germans until reinforcements could arrive. About the bullet wound he suffered while crawling to aid a bleeding soldier. About the last scene he remembered as he was taken from the gory place called Ardennes, what I would later learn was the Battle of the Bulge.

When he finished, he reached into his shirt pocket, the one always buttoned, and took out two medals. One was purple and shaped like a heart. The other was a gold star. On his yellow palm they shined brightly in the sunlight. Speechless, I touched one then the other, moving my fingers over them lightly, as though they possessed some kind of magic.

Looking up at him, I said, "I'm gonna be like you."

"Say what?"

"When I grow up, I'm gonna be a preacher."

His hands fumbled as he put the medals back into his pocket and re-buttoned it. "You gonna be like me 'cause o' what I done told you? Preachers don't kill. Killin' is wrong. Forget 'bout them medals," Then, he mumbled to himself, "Shouldn't've shone 'em to you in the first place."

"But, Uncle Giles, you saved people."

He just looked at me, his astonished face running with sweat, but said nothing. He slapped the reins and the wagon moved on.

*   *   *

The light was still red. I continued looking at the poster then saw what I'd not glimpsed at first. It *was* Uncle Sam all right, holding in one hand the familiar decorated red and white-striped stovepipe hat, the other hand outthrust, a finger pointing. Bold letters at the top said, I WANT YOU, all right. But the rest was not all right. The rest was chilling. This Uncle Sam wore a white hooded-robe with a red cross over his heart, and the caption at the bottom read ...

In The
WHITE KNIGHTS
Of MISSISSIPPI
KU KLUX KLAN

... and I was suddenly reminded this was the land of the Klan.

I began to feel its incorrigible pressure, the heart of its dark past still there, beating like an old drum, ready to march one more time.

The light finally changed and I turned. The thin macadam, eroding along the shoulders, barely resembled a highway but a sign a mile or so out said 440, so I drove on through deep woods, encroaching brush and kudzu that tumbled toward the road, a dark leafy tunnel that allowed little sunlight. The lane I traveled grew spookier and I thought again of the poster. I'd been born and raised in Mississippi. I had hunted in its forests and its Appalachian foothills, in places called Twenty Mile Bottom, Hatchie Hills, Hell Creek. But I'd never seen woods like these, one continuous matted jungle.

Occasional breaks in the dense foliage allowed views of fields mired with rusting machinery, the gutted wreckage of a battle lost, a war still raging against boll weevils, heat and dust ... and time. Small clapboard houses with crippled porches and junky yards swept by, their collapsed barns and sheds a testament to their poverty. I had the feeling everything I saw was broken off from something larger, grander and long forgotten. Once in a while, I'd see a church. For most folks, it was the only symbol of hope around. Many of these people were the poor whites, vestiges of a war a hundred years old whose grandparents allowed the politicians to convince them blacks were their enemy and sent a message in the hinge election of 1896 when the South turned Democrat and became "The Solid South." Now, it was 1964 and Barry Goldwater was trying to reverse the politics. George Wallace might help him. For the first time in their family's heritage, many would vote Republican.

Several miles from Mt. Pleasant, I saw, for the first time, the Mississippi Delta. As though by some sudden geological fault, the land dropped, and the corridor of trees fell away. The sky opened up, and in the hazy distance I beheld, as straight as if laid down by a ruler, the horizon. All the way to its rim, flat and undefiled, the valley floor extended. The road I traveled slid downward onto that vast green plain, and I had the eerie feeling I was descending into some strange and forbidden land more foreign than the stories I'd heard, more alien than the descriptions I'd read.

Over the even and uniform country and into the late level sunlight I sailed, my eyes drawn left and right to the straight rows of green cotton as they flicked by. For miles, I saw no houses, not one. Just cotton. Occasionally, amid a copse of trees, I'd see a clump of shacks where surely no one lived. Today, there is limited cotton in the Mississippi Delta. Mostly soybean and rice fields and catfish ponds. But at that time, all I saw was a green ocean of cotton, a plant that yielded a white substance that told the tale of this part of the world.

One of the churches and my parsonage for the summer seminary internship were located in Mount Pleasant. But Brother Fabian Allshouse, the senior pastor of the church charge, was waiting for me in nearby Waverley, Mississippi.

Brother Allshouse's wife met me at the door and ushered me into the study. Brother Allshouse was a tall, fullback stock of man with distinguished graying temples and a pug nose. He had a stiff formality about him and was wearing heavy spectacles. He hiked his mouth to one side when he spoke and, in a pronounced rural accent, said he was glad to see me. He settled into a leather chair behind his desk and I sat uneasily in a large rocker across from him. He told me the general order of things. He told me what was and was not expected of me. Keeping the parsonage clean and the lawn mowed were at the top of the list.

"The parsonage ladies have informed me they kept pots and pans and silverware in the kitchen," he said. "Just the basics, you understand, so you may have to drum up anything else you want or need. Just mention it from the pulpit."

Next on his list came regular visitation, daily to those in the area hospitals. I was expected to preach five times each Sunday, alternating congregations every other Sunday so I never preached twice in a row at the same church. Except at Mount Pleasant. I was to preach there every Sunday at the eleven o'clock service. I did catch a break. Wednesday evening prayer meetings had been postponed for the summer to resume after Labor Day, when I'd be back in school.

Thanks to my parents' discipline growing up, I knew how to mow a lawn, clean a house and keep a kitchen spotless. I'd conducted worship services, preached a few times. I'd visited in homes and hospitals. So far, so good.

"Now, you may have a funeral or two," Brother Allshouse added, "and the congregations expect communion on the first Sunday of each month."

I had never consoled the bereaved or buried their dead, thoughts still as awesome and terrifying now, after forty years, as they were then. Dying and death never get easy. I had assisted with communion in the seminary chapel, but I was not yet ordained. Only ordained elders were vested with the authority to conduct Holy Communion.

"All I have is a license to preach," I said to him apologetically. "I'm not ordained. How can I serve communion?"

"You can serve communion as long as you're under my direction and authority," he responded. "*The Discipline* allows for that."

The Discipline. I'd forgotten about *The Discipline*, that little black book that is to Methodism what *The Torah* is to Judaism.

"What about weddings?" I said.

"Either I or Brother Garland Hammingtree, the District Superintendent, will cover those."

He then gave me telephone numbers and a recent map of the area. He called out the names of the churches—Waverley, Mount Pleasant, Lebanon, Beulah Grove, Mars Hill, Mount Nebo, Mount Pisgah, Mount Hebron, Mount Zion, Salem—a recitation that sounded like something from Bible Geography 101. Until he said, "and Redbone."

"Redbone?"

"Nobody knows why it's called that," he said, "Maybe you'll find out. Let me know if you do."

He swiveled in his chair and looked out the window. His brain seemed to be working in his jaws where tiny muscles fanned into the graying undergrowth of his thick sideburns. I was on the verge of asking a question about the poster I'd seen when he swiveled back around.

"And another thing," he continued. "Don't preach on anything controversial. Stay away from race, sex and politics."

I nodded, but wondered what was left. What he said next bolted me upright.

"You've got to handle that Mount Pleasant bunch with kid gloves. A lot of 'em are in the Klan. They don't cotton to anything that smacks of lib'ralism." He was choosing his words carefully, avoiding the word "integration." I wondered then, and still do, where the phrase "cotton to" came from. I knew it meant "to like" or "get along with" something or someone quickly or easily. But cotton? Cotton was the reason for so much dislike and discord in that neck of the woods. In the entire South. The country. A civil war was fought over it.

"How many of them are in the Klan?" I said.

"Nobody knows. They wear hoods, you know. We haven't had too much of a problem with 'em here, but they've been stirring up things over in Greenwood." He paused, his eyes steady on me as if assessing my reaction.

My body tensed and I wondered if he could sense my rising anxiety. Greenwood was where the all-white Citizens Council was formed ten years before. Near Greenwood was Itta Bena where fourteen year-old Emmett Till was lynched the next year.

He continued. "But then we haven't had any of those freedom riders over here. Not yet, anyhow. Let's hope to God they stay in Greenwood and keep the Klan busy over there. That's all we need, somebody stirring up these law-abiding nigras over here. I just preach the Lord's word and shepherd my people. I'd advise you to do the same."

There was more I wanted to say, especially about the "Lord's word," but I let him continue. He was winding down.

"Of course, we've got a big potluck supper tonight at the Waverley church. The entire charge will be there. Everybody wants to meet the new young preacher. They sent great news of you from seminary. Ruth Stowes thinks you hung the moon, says you're the best preacher to come down the pike in years."

I cannot recall if I thanked him for the compliment. I was still hung up on the supper. No one had told me about a charge supper. It wasn't factored into my plans. Supper meant it would be dark when I arrived back in Mount Pleasant, a discomforting prospect, moving into the parsonage at night. No one seemed to have taken that concern into consideration.

The potluck supper was a festive rendition of dinner-on-the-grounds. People sat in folding chairs beneath huge oaks. Children ran and chased each other. Several teenagers played softball at one end of the church's large yard. Men talked quietly in small groups near the trees. Some remained at their cars or pickups, their feet propped on fenders, smoking or dipping snuff. Several women stood whisking away flies with paper plates over the food arranged on two long rows of white linen-covered tables. The scene was a familiar one, nothing unusual or out of the ordinary.

All of the churches of the Waverley circuit were represented. I was the new preacher, at least for the summer, and everybody took a shot at charming me. A few, that day, stood out.

Dorsey Dance of Mars Hill was a small man with a thin nose, droopy colorless mustache beneath it and a round, almost featureless, head. He had a crafty smile and a laugh that had a sharp edge. He grew the biggest tomatoes in the county and said I would always have a supply of them. And I did, huge, bright red ones, piled up past the wire handle of the fruit basket he always left on the parsonage side-door stoop.

"Red" Kilmichael of Lebanon was a refreshing surprise. He had a rugged, angular face that could have been cut from granite and a character to match. He hooked his hand in the crook of my arm, took me over under a shady oak and told me he had the best coon dogs in the country and would take me on coon hunts. If I had any trouble with the Waverley folks or Brother Allshouse to let him know and he'd threaten to pull his money out of the conference "askings," a move that would put the church and Brother Allshouse on the bishop's blacklist. "Mr. Red," as I learned to affectionately call him, was one of the smartest people I'd ever known. I relearned so much I had forgotten in Scouts about how to survive and find my way out of thick forests and what I could and couldn't eat in the process. He also taught me something about people, our misperceptions and misjudgments of them, our faulty stereotyping and how knowing the difference could mean everything, including life or death.

I recall one other memorable character that evening.

"You ain't one of them radicals, them outside agitators, are ye?" a man said eyeing me keenly. He identified himself simply as Hunsucker from Redbone. No Mister. No first name. Just Hunsucker. I learned later that everyone called him Top. His voice had a quavering, high whiney pitch, the sound of a child's with age. He was tall, raw-boned and broad shouldered with a clay-colored face on a large round head that reminded me of Hoss on Bonanza. He had crooked yellow teeth. And his blue eyes were puffy and bloodshot, deep set in folds of fat, which gave the appearance of a constant squint. He was moving his tongue around in his mouth as if trying to dislodge a piece of food caught between his teeth. His height drew my eyes upward, and he was still pumping my hand when I smiled at him and responded. "No sir. Not on your life."

He nodded. Then nodded again. For a long time, it seemed, he stood there, his eyes assessing me. Then he pursed meaty lips into a slow mischievous grin, backed one step away and said, "That's good. You wouldn't last long 'round here if you was." He winked, but there was a gleam in his narrow eyes, like a warning.

While the ladies cleared the tables, a hymn was sung by all—*Standing on the Promises.* Brother Allshouse arose and formally introduced me. He spoke glowing words and went on and on. Heads nodded and smiled as if the accomplishments were materializing before their eyes and I sensed a linkage with the hymn, that the promises were stacking up.

When he finished, the sun had moved lower in the sky. I was anxious to head back to Mount Pleasant, but knew the bases that had to be covered, the hands I needed to shake and the women I needed to thank for all the food.

Soon, Brother Allshouse put his arm around my shoulder and walked me to my car.

"You call me if you need anything now, you hear?" he said.

I assured him I would.

2

Leaving the Delta, the road bowed upward and rose steeply. The sun's rays were orange in the tops of the trees as I crested the ancient bluffs, the sacerdotal watchtowers of the long-removed Choctaws. Through the rearview mirror the sun appeared, a blood-red disc beneath a dark band of clouds riding atop thin, saffron streaks and flickering with veins of lightening. A low thick mist covered the land, heightening the brooding effect. I refocused on the road ahead. I wanted to reach Mount Pleasant before dark, ahead of the ominous storm following me.

Tall trees cathedraled over the road as I drove through black flat walls of immense woods. A sultry wind rushing through the windows seemed to suck me deeper into a corridor of darkness.

You ain't one of them radicals, them outside agitators, are ye?

No sir, not on your life.

"I should have said not on *my* life," I murmured to myself. His name was Hunsucker, and I pondered the surname's origin. I wondered if it was Germanic or a bastardization, a fusing, of some backwoods creation. His being from Redbone suggested the latter.

The sun had set and storm clouds were moving in, but there was still enough light to see the parsonage. Set among similar dwellings with larger grounds, it was a simple frame structure placed inside a medium-sized yard. Two square wooden columns bracketed a small gallery around the front door. Barely visible beneath uncut grass and weeds, a buckled sidewalk led to front steps that listed to one side. Across the front, overgrown hydrangeas and nandinas extended in a bushy array. Shingles were missing from the roof. Some had lost their hold from age and neglect and slipped into crinkled gutters engorged with leaves.

I turned into the drive and pulled under the carport. A utility room was located at the back. Its door was unlocked and inside, as Brother Allshouse had instructed, was the most significant article, besides a car, a Methodist preacher should possess: a lawnmower. When a preacher is ordained into the United Methodist Church, as it is called now, he or she is still asked, in keeping with John Wesley's original *Discipline*, if they own a horse. It would be appropriate to add ownership of a lawnmower.

The key to the side door of the house fit easily, and I entered cautiously. The air was dank and muggy, the smell moldy. I found a light switch and quickly began going room-to-room, turning on lights, opening windows, hammering along their sides with my fists where they were stuck. More than anything, the place needed some fresh air.

Everything was as Brother Allshouse had described. The furniture was intact, the number of pieces and their condition as he had reported. A little lumpy but functional, the bed looked as though it had been freshly made. The hardwood floors had been polished, and the linoleum in the kitchen and bathroom, though warped and curling around the edges, had a clean shine. I found the silverware and cooking utensils in the kitchen, more than Brother Allshouse had estimated. Adjacent to the stove, a small refrigerator yielded several items including quarts of orange juice and milk, a carton of eggs and a loaf of Wonder Bread.

I unloaded the car just as the wind began gusting. High up, the tops of the trees leaned at severe angles and along the street, leaves and paper scraps blew. The air was heavy with the unmistakable smell of an imminent downpour. Lightning popped nearby and hurried me along.

It didn't take long for me to put up clothes, arrange books and set up my stereo. There was no radio or television, which I had not expected. No shower either. Only an old-fashioned enameled tub on claw-feet, brown iron stains around the fixtures.

The bath revived me and I decided to put on some classical music. I picked through the handful of albums I'd packed and decided Dvorak's

New World Symphony was appropriate. The night had crumbled into a prolonged storm, and the rain was coming down hard. Runoff from the roof splattered loudly around the edge of the house. Lightning flashes and thunder rolls counterpointed the plaintive horns and tympani of the symphony's *adagio*. I envisioned the famous Czech writing while listening to a storm as it moved across the Iowan plains.

I turned off the lights and sat looking out the window into the melancholy night. In the downpour, I saw a lone black man atop a mule-drawn wagon moving slowly through pools of streetlight. I thought of Giles, my black mentor, shepherd, the man responsible for my being where I was and I recalled the first time I had met him.

* * *

I was ten years old and playing jacks on the sidewalk in front of my house on Cleveland Street in New Albany, Mississippi. It was one of those perfect days. A cool and gentle breeze was blowing beneath a cloudless sky. I heard a distant rumbling, like faraway thunder. It grew louder as it rattled and clanked with clip-clopping sounds and a wagon came into view. Sitting atop the wagon was a black man wearing a white shirt and a brimmed hat. The stump of a cigar jutted from the side of his mouth. The wagon kept coming until it was almost on top of me. The man pulled back on the reins, and the wagon came to a stop. The man thumbed his hat back on his head and held the reins lax in his lap. "Hidy-do," he said to me.

I said, "Hidy," then, "My name's Sammy. Who are you?"

"His name is Giles Word."

The voice came from behind me. I turned and saw my mother standing on the porch, her hands propped atop a broom handle.

"Afternoon, Miss Joan," the man said doffing his hat, then returning it to its jaunty tilt. "Hadn't seen you in a coon's age."

"You're a sight for sore eyes yourself, Uncle Giles," my mother said.

"Yessum. Been a while."

"Whose uncle is he?" I asked, then impolitely blurted, "Ain't mine."

My mother and the man named Uncle Giles laughed.

"It's a long story. Uncle Giles is like part of our family, a long lost part," my mother said, looking up seriously at Giles. "He worked for your granddaddy, on the old place in the country then was called to preach."

Giles nodded and smiled. "I was just a young'un then."

I was listening.

"What brings you back our way?" my mother said.

"Gotta get this load of slab to Miss Bostwick's. This here's my wagon, but I'm working for the sawmill hauling slab wood. You mind if Mister Sammy rides with me, Miss Joan? Won't be gone long. Just a couple of blocks."

"He'd love that, Giles," she said. "I know you'll take good care of him."

Before she could change her mind, I was scrambling up the hardwood spokes, over the steel-rimmed wheels and into the wagon. As we pulled away, Giles was clucking, "Giddyup, Bud, giddyup," as he rippled the reins across the mule's smooth back. What I did not know in that moment, had no inkling, was that the ride I was taking—*Won't be gone long*—was just the beginning of a long sojourn into a world of stories and lore that played themselves out in dialogues of extraordinary companionship. It was also the beginning of a big turn my life would take.

The last time I saw Giles, I was at home preparing for college. I don't recall the exact time except it was winter, sometime after Christmas. I remember it was cold and raining heavily. I was in the living room where the windows faced the street. The drapes were pulled back. It was raining so hard all I could hear was the downpour drumming like a prolonged and steady thunder on the roof and against the windowpanes. Through that heavy gray deluge, I saw something dark coming slowly down the street. I got up from the floor where I had spread some scholarship applications I'd been completing and went to one of the windows. Closer and closer it came, this apparition in slow motion, this ghostly image distorted by the slight warp in the glass and by the rain. Soon, my eyes began to make out a black mule and black wagon. It was Giles; it couldn't be anyone else.

A black hooded rain slicker was tented over him like a poncho so it covered his hands, giving the appearance that the reins were being held by something invisible. His head was bowed. A black tarpaulin fanned out behind him to cover his load. I thought hearse, one of another era, as the mule, wagon and crouched driver passed the front of the house, moving slowly, pane by pane, through the windows. My mother entered the room and looked with me. "Oh my," she said sadly, "Giles out there in this kind of weather. He'll catch his death." That was in 1960. I never saw him again. At least, not for a very long time.

*   *   *

The wagon disappeared, and the night grew quiet. I turned off the lights and climbed between sheets that crinkled with meticulous cleanliness and care. Rain-cooled breezes blew randomly through the slightly opened window. Branches scraped against the screens. Lightning bugs blinked against the black of the trees. Cicadas whirred. Whippoorwills strobed. An owl moaned. The only other sounds were those of distant thunder and the slow soft rain like a thousand ticking clocks and I closed my eyes and went to sleep.

3

Monday, July 6

The first few weeks I'd been so engaged in my new responsibilities and challenges, I'd almost forgotten that this was a summer internship for which I would receive credits and that a thesis on my experience was due upon my return in August. Despite the delay from my arrival, I began keeping a journal.

My routine involved going first to the Mount Pleasant Church each morning to check my mail. The parsonage had no box, so any mail coming to me would be in the receptacle at the church.

One morning, a dust-coated, late model Chevrolet station wagon was parked in front of the church. It had an Ohio license plate. I assumed someone had parked to use the rest room at Ivy Lee Jessup's gas station across the street or was lost and trying to get directions. I saw no sign of human life in or around the car.

I entered the side door of the church where there was a small office. The door was never locked. Except for the antiquated mimeograph machine for anyone with the time and strength to carry it off, there was nothing of worth to steal.

The office was empty, but I could hear voices coming from the sanctuary. I tiptoed to a side door, turned the knob slowly to make a crack and peaked in. Two male figures were standing close together at the chancel in the cool dark of the sanctuary. One was pointing toward the choir loft and then moved his arm in an arc toward the back of the church, as though making a point to the other about the architecture.

"May I help you?" I interrupted.

Both jumped. "Good afternoon," they said jointly as they turned to face me. One was bald and had a neatly trimmed beard. The other was almost bald and wore wire-rimmed glasses. Both were tall and slender and fit together well in their lankiness.

"My name's James Brodsky," said the bearded one.

"And I'm Eli Rubin," said the other. "Hope we're not intruding. We were looking for the pastor. The door was open so we let ourselves in."

Their accents were decidedly northern. Soft, mid-west northern Ohio, like the license plate said.

"We were just admiring your sanctuary," said the one named Brodsky, gesturing again with an upward sweep of his arm. "How old is this church?"

"Parts of it are over a hundred years old," I said. "It was built before the Civil War but has undergone several restorations. To be honest, I don't know when any of the changes or additions began. But thanks for your compliment. I'll pass it along. And you're not intruding." I wanted to be polite, but I was feeling uneasy. Their car tag spelled trouble. "I'm Sam. I'm the pastor."

We approached and shook hands. They said I looked too young to be the pastor. I told them I was the assistant pastor of an eleven church circuit on summer work scholarship assignment. Summer seemed to be the pitch word, and they told me about their seasonal assignment. Brodsky was with the Student Non-Violent Coordinating Committee (SNCC). Rubin was working for COFO, translated Council of Federated Organizations. I was familiar with SNCC because of their activity on the Emory campus in Atlanta. COFO I'd not heard about. Rubin described it as a tent under which all of the major civil rights organizations were working together in Mississippi. The main office was in Jackson, but their field headquarters were in Greenwood, in adjacent Leflore County. Their designated project was canvassing Negro residences in Holmes County in preparation for a voter registration drive. Another phase of the project included setting up and operating freedom schools and building community centers for the Negroes. They already had a ten thousand dollar gift from a wealthy donor in California. More was sure to come. Their eyes flashed with confidence, a look I recall with absolute clarity.

"We wanted to introduce ourselves to the clergy in the area," Rubin said. "Especially the Methodists. We've learned you're more progressive than the others and might be willing to help us."

The hook was carefully set. *Help* was the key word, but *progressive* the one that resonated. I'd returned to my home state to help, but by working within the system. Their emphasis on progressive suggested otherwise. I recalled something a seminary professor—Dr. Manfred Hoffman, church history—had told me about establishment and anti-establishment forces, their similarities to laws of physics. Centripetal force draws inward toward the center. Centrifugal pulls or flies outward. The trick for anyone wanting to effect change in a system, any system, Dr. Hoffman had said, was to hang in the lip between the two forces. Not get sucked in and lose identity. And not get thrown out and lose leverage. I was barely settling into that "lip between the two," and thought I'd just been asked to choose one or the other. I was too young to be an insider, part of the establishment. I was no crusader, certainly not a martyr. I was not particularly courageous, though I picked up a little pluck here and there along the way. I had kept my distance from the anti-war and civil rights protest movements in Atlanta and sensed I should do the same here.

"I'm not sure how I could be of help to you," I said.

They looked at each other before Brodsky spoke. I'd decided he was the spokesman for the two. "Our canvassers need food, a place to rest and refresh, toilet facilities. Some will travel from other locations, as far away as Jackson, and will need a central meeting point, a place to park their cars. Of course, any donations would be appreciated, but we don't ask for those."

These were reasonable requests, but I hesitated. A Negro C.M.E. church had been burned the week before and the area was simmering like a boiling pot, the lid about to blow. The Civil Rights Act of 1964 was only a few days old, almost a year since President Kennedy had given his televised speech about the historic legislation. According to recent news reports, the summer was not going well for the Movement. In only a few places were victories achieved. The NAACP integrated local hotels in Jackson, the state capitol, without any major incidents. On their own, individuals made inroads. In Greenville, a hundred plus took the voter registration test without arrests. Thirty picketed in Cleveland without incident. J. Edgar Hoover personally opened the Jackson FBI office, the first statewide center since 1946, and boasted about its hundred and fifty-three agents. Many saw in his action the turn in the long road to freedom. Then came the detour. He announced the FBI could give "no protection" to civil rights workers.

So much for the Civil Rights Act of 1964. The law was one thing, enforcement another.

In the days following the law's enactment, terror reigned. Bombed: a freedom house in McComb and a Negro cafe in Vicksburg. Torched: Mount Zion Hill Baptist Church in Pike County and Bovina Community Center. At Browning, the Pleasant Ridge Missionary Church burned to the ground; Negroes wouldn't sell to whites who sought to buy it. At a voter rally in Moss Point, while singing "We Shall Overcome," a Negro woman was shot twice. A gas bomb was tossed at a local Negro's home in Laurel. Twenty-five in Drew were arrested for "willfully and unlawfully" using the sidewalks and streets during a voter registration rally. Everywhere, volunteers were arrested without cause: for taking photos in a courtroom; for putting posters on a telephone pole; for refusing to cross the street when ordered by police; for trespassing at a gas station to stop and buy a soft drink; for public profanity, overheard by a policeman to say "damn;" reckless driving. For these offenses, blacks and freedom riders were jailed, fined and often beaten before release.

Closer to Mount Pleasant, there was more of the same. On July fifth, a much-heralded NAACP delegation landed in Jackson. The same day, Silas McGhee, a twenty-one year-old black, led a one-man crusade to desegregate the Leflore Theater in Greenwood. People had talked about how he walked down the street in his paratrooper uniform like Wyatt Earp headed for the O. K. Corral. Once inside the theater and in his seat, he was jumped by fifteen white men and beaten. He went back seven more times in the month, walking through picket lines where one Byron De La Beckwith shouted jeers and insults. When the editor of the *Greenwood Commonwealth* crossed the picket lines with his family, his home received threatening phone calls, followed by rifle shots.

From the media and from gossip, I knew these facts and thought about them as I continued facing the two men. If I said yes, did it mean I became an initiate of The Movement and have its troops camping in the churchyard? I had returned to the state to make a difference, albeit in my own small way, but I knew the outcry from my parishioners that would surely follow. I would become labeled as "one of them radicals." I considered myself neither prepared nor ready to travel that road. I thought back on Dr. Hoffman's metaphor. If I were going to effect any change, I'd have to work both sides of the fence. I needed to know more about the other side. "I'm sure you know what you're asking me to do, the risks involved," I said to them.

Rubin and Brodsky nodded. Rubin spoke this time. "But if we don't ask, we don't receive. And we come to the churches first because"—he nodded toward the chancel and a large cross on the altar—"risk is what it's all about."

The irony did not escape me, a Jew making reference to the cross. The Jews had certainly had their own crosses to bear over the centuries. That irrefutable logic aside, I pondered his use of the impersonal pronoun. I still wasn't sure what *it* was. "If I'm going to make that kind of decision, I need to know more about you. How do I know you are who you say you are?"

"Fair enough," Brodsky said. "Come to one of our meetings."

"Where do you hold them?"

"Do you know where Bethel Church is on the Acona road?" Rubin said. "Where it used to be, rather. It was burned several days ago by nightriders."

"Yes. I'd heard it was burned," I said.

Rubin continued. "If you're driving toward Acona, there's a Negro Baptist church about five miles from there. It's called Mount Holy Rest."

I knew exactly where it was. I turned there to go to Redbone. "Yes. The road is on my charge circuit."

"Great!" Brodsky exclaimed beaming. "We hold meetings there every Wednesday evening, starting at seven o'clock. You could probably come any night and find us. There's a lot going on."

Rubin jumped in. "This Wednesday night would be a good time to come. Reverend Ed King from Jackson will be there with a group from

Tougaloo College. He's bringing some of the freedom chaplains with him. Great opportunity for you to meet them."

Somehow, instead of a Wednesday evening prayer meeting, I knew this was going to be a "come to Jesus" meeting, but a different Jesus than the one I'd been raised knowing. Meeting freedom chaplains was not at the top of my list of things to do. My marching orders, per Mrs. Stowes and Brother Allshouse, were to preach on Sundays and to visit the sick and shut-ins and each church family during my short summer tenure. That left little time for anything else. In that moment, I wished I'd had a Wednesday evening prayer meeting to lead. I wished for an excuse.

I forget the dialogue at this point because I heard a door open and shut behind the sanctuary. With someone about to break in on the scene, I hastened an end to the discussion, shook hands with the two emissaries and ushered them out the front door. As I turned to reenter the sanctuary, Mrs. Abston, the secretary, entered from a door at the back.

"Who were those folks?" she said.

"Just a couple of men traveling through. They thought the church was pretty, wanted to take a look at it."

Applying Dr. Hoffman's metaphor of physics, like an iron filing I flew to the magnet's core.

I wondered about the bishop's policy regarding his ministers' involvement in the Civil Rights movement. He was of the old school and became a bishop, as most did, because he could preach and was a politician. Whether or not he had any grasp for administration and polity, no one had said. The word in seminary was he ruled with an iron fist, meaning preachers were expected to attend all meetings and ensure their churches met conference "askings," especially those earmarked for the World Council of Churches. I'd heard nothing about extracurricular activities.

I decided to call Brother Allshouse, but try an oblique approach. After reporting to him Monday on Sunday's attendance figures and collection intakes, and before closing the conversation, I asked if he'd heard about any preachers attending civil rights gatherings. The sound of a seltzer bottle suddenly uncorked and exploding through the receiver might best describe his reaction.

"About what? Do what?"

I attempted to repeat my question, but he cut me off.

"Heck no, I hadn't heard of any. 'Cause they know if they did they'd get their name on the Citizens Council's blacklist. They'd circulate it around the state, then the Klan would get it and before you know it, they'd end up like those three in Philadelphia, missing or dead. No sirreebob, I hadn't heard of any and I don't want to hear of any. The bishop has told us to keep the peace and stay in our place and extend brotherly love and to do it quietly."

That was all he said. Caesar's orders to Pilate came to mind: Keep the lid on and the temple tax flowing. Brother Allshouse didn't ask why I wanted to know, but the brief homily I'd received suggested he knew.

4

Wednesday, July 8

That evening, the sun was setting as I backed out of the parsonage drive. Due to the July 4th holiday, many of my church members were away. I took a paved county road west to Blackhawk where I turned south onto a wider paved state road, then five miles before the Acona city limits veered back southeast onto a gravel road. Through thick woods and long shadows, I drove. Regardless of a person's point of origin, in Holmes County, Mississippi, clear skies or cloudy, new moon or full, he soon traveled a corridor of curtained darkness.

Cooler evening air swept through the windows. Gravel splaying from the tires popped and pinged the undercarriage. Occasionally, branches brushed the top and sides of the car and thrummed the antenna. The road narrowed and washboarded so that at times it could have been a logging trail. I thought of one I traversed once with Giles and his comment: "That county supervisor got mo' important things to do than maintain this here right o' way." He went on to postulate scripture about narrow ways and small gates, drawing one more positive lesson from a simple negative.

I was having less luck.

A rare stretch of countryside suddenly opened up. Distant lights backlit the low hills and treetops and cones of light from my car scoped the road. Frequently, I checked the rearview. I knew Brother Allshouse was right. I needed to be concerned about people checking tags. That was a well-known tactic of the Klan and the Citizens Council. He was right, too, about lists of tags and car makes circulating in the state. The Citizens Council wielded more power than the Klan. Its members came from respectable circles of power. Some of my church members belonged to both.

My hands tightened on the steering wheel and began to sweat. I thought again about my decision and why I'd made it and questioned if I should not turn back. For the past few days, I'd had nightmares where members of my congregations tailed me. They wore white hooded robes and stood around a burning cross while drawing straws. Visions of Molotov cocktails spreading streams of fire in the parsonage and bombs blowing out windows lit up the dark corners of my sleep. In one dream, a parishioner arose in church and challenged my whereabouts. Another joined him and cited my license number. I awoke shouting, "No! No! No!" The scene happened at the Redbone church. I remembered that, too.

I looked down and checked my clothes again. White shirt. No tie. Navy blue blazer. Brown Loafers. Not too formal, not too informal. Not impressive but not unimpressive. Neutral. Except I was not neutral. I was white and most in the audience would be black.

I passed the burned C.M.C. Bethel Church, its roofless crypt and blackened beams projecting into the moonless air like the tortured charcoal drawing of a school child. Since time began, they had been called sanctuaries, places of refuge, of safety. As the road curved and entered again another tunnel of woods, I thought about that, the names of sanctuaries and how they came to be. Bethel. Beth-el, Hebrew for "House of God," second to Jerusalem, the place mentioned more often in scripture than any other. Abraham pitched his tent and built his first altar there. Jacob, the one who named it, had his ladder dream of angels and revelation of God there. Over the centuries, in one fashion or another, Israelite leaders, one after the other, paid homage to the sacred altar. Over time, place defined the name. Bethel, the place where such and such happened, where so and so worshipped and so and so passed through. Now, Bethel, the place where niggers worship. Burn her down.

A few more miles and I saw Mount Holy Rest, its steeple stamped on the night. Mount Holy Rest, another interesting name which had, I was sure, an equally interesting history. The church grounds were covered with cars and trucks and a few mule-drawn wagons. I could have easily parked on the road's shoulder, but my tag would be sticking out like an invitation, so I pulled into the yard and weaved my way to a spot under a large tree between a pickup and a wagon, very similar to the one I rode in with Giles.

I turned off the ignition and pulled the hand break. The small wooden church was brightly lit, people standing around the windows and in the door. Festive sounds of singing and clapping filled the night air. I rolled up the windows and sat for a few minutes. The singing and clapping sounded farther away, like a distant pep rally.

I listened, second-guessing if I should not have parked closer to the road.

I looked around for signs of note takers. One man was leaning against a wagon, but he was black and probably taking care of the rig and watching the animal. It was not too late to back out, but I had squirmed my way into a nearly irreversible parking position. Backing out would be a feat. I pulled up the lock and opened the car door. The air was warm and heavy, rich with the odor of cedar and pine.

I felt my way through the parked vehicles and moved slowly across the grounds, stepping high to avoid tripping on roots. Singing and clapping poured through the open windows and doors. I climbed the steps. A dog with gray stubble around his muzzle was curled up on the landing. He seemed lulled into sleep by the din and could probably sleep through a battle. The front doors were opened back on both sides. I stopped and leaned against the jamb of one and beheld the wild, ecstatic scene inside.

A large black man was standing behind the pulpit leading the singing. He was waving his arms and behind him swayed a choir of adults and children, all sizes, all shades of their color. On the dais to the right of the song leader was a white minister. Standing beside the song leader, he looked thin and anemic. By his white clerical collar, he was either Episcopal or Roman Catholic.

A man at the door motioned me in. Several toward the back turned around and noted me with curious eyes. I found a vacant spot along the back wall between two tall Negro men and slipped into it. I felt like a period between exclamation points.

I checked my watch. The crowd had been going about thirty minutes. As I had expected, most were black. A few whites sat on the front row. I counted ten. Two sitting side by side appeared to be James Brodsky and Eli Rubin. They turned their heads. I was right. They hadn't seen me, but I was hoping they might. Any familiar face would be a comfort.

The crowd was singing a song I'd never heard. I felt uncomfortable not joining in but would have felt more uncomfortable trying, so I just stood and watched … and listened.

Oh, oh Freedom
Oh, oh Freedom,
Oh, oh Freedom over me, over me
And before I'll be a slave,
I'll be buried in my grave,
And go home to my Lord and be free.

The singing stopped and the white minister stepped to the pulpit. He was not introduced. He said he was from Tougaloo College and was there to introduce two chaplains who would be working in the area for the next month with the freedom task force. He called their names and asked them to stand. David Osler from Columbus, Ohio, and Derrick Rutherford from Albany, New York. Both stood and turned to rousing applauses and "Amen!"s and "Yes, Brother!"s. The white priest went on to explain their job was to be minister-counselors to volunteers in the projects, but they would also be working with local clergy as much as possible. *As much as possible.* I thought about that and wondered how much, if any, would be possible for me, for I felt the pressure of the moment, the heat bearing down.

The next speaker rose. He was black and had been seated on the dais behind the pulpit. In the flutter of fans, I didn't catch his name and never saw him again after that night. He was tall and lean, straight-backed with a round head that looked like a small ball perched above his flattened shoulders and his long arms stretched beyond his sleeves. He was introduced as one of the project leaders. His voice was intelligent. He began by stating the reason for the meeting and those to follow. He laid out broad-brush plans and strategies of things to come. He spoke with pride about the freedom school that was ready to begin and the curriculum, how black children would learn more than just reading, writing and arithmetic, that they would learn black history, story writing, expression of feelings, drama, singing, poetry. They would learn to understand democracy and tyranny and the difference, and how to register to vote, to memorize the parts of the Mississippi Constitution required by the law of this state in order to vote, and how to answer the other complex questions required. He said the schools would flourish regardless of recent laws passed by the white Mississippi legislature outlawing them.

If the churches were burned, they would study in the sheds.

If the sheds were burned, they would study in the storefronts and lodge halls.

If those were burned, they would go on studying in the fields.

The schools would be everywhere—Jackson, McComb, Tchula, Clarksdale, Hattiesburg, Indianola, Tupelo, Philadelphia, and on and on. His delivery was that of a preacher as his voice pitched higher and arms gestured, his eyes rolling and flashing with vision. He moved with confidence in himself and his place in the world. He removed his coat and rolled up his sleeves. His long arms glistened under the glare of the high ceiling lights. Sweat ran down his face. He spoke with well-measured words and long pauses. He spoke with the arrogance of a man who could face any odds.

I looked at the people. I looked back at the speaker. I felt an energy flowing between them, one that touched me. I trembled as I listened to his dream and looked around me at a people getting ready to take their first trip to the moon.

I was captivated.

No.

I was inspired.

The speaker continued and moved to other topics. There was something in the tone of his voice I found intoxicating. He took his handkerchief and wrapped it around his hand and jabbed at the air. I heard names that still remain with me. He spoke of Martin Luther King, Jr. and his dream, of Medgar Evers and his undying devotion and sacrifice and of Fanny Lou Hamer, the Movement's David going out to meet Goliath. When the name Rosa Parks left his lips, a loud chorus struck the air. Other names followed, each with a murmur of approval from the crowd. His rising tone and his content turned vitriolic on others—J. Edgar Hoover (who had recently called Martin Luther King the most notorious liar in the country), George Wallace, the Kennedys for not promising protection in '63 and Lyndon Johnson for not promising it now. The one name not mentioned was the speaker's. It would be given to me later. Stokely Carmichael.

When he finished, the crowd sang a song I knew, "This Little Light of Mine." Caught up in the fervor, I found myself singing and clapping with the others.

Following the singing, James Brodsky turned and noticed me. I saw him stand and motion to the priest on the dais. The priest rose and walked to the edge of the crowded platform and nodded as Brodsky spoke in his ear and gestured toward the back with his arm. Both looked in my direction. The priest nodded again. He'd be glad to make the introduction, I guessed. Wrong. His strong voice called upon James Brodsky, Holmes County project co-director, to introduce a special guest.

Brodsky stepped onto the dais. "Good people. I want you to know there is a man of courage among us tonight."

"Yes, Brother!" shouted one.

"Amen!" followed another.

"Eli Rubin and I met him last week. He's the summer pastor of Mount Pleasant Methodist Church. Let's give a big freedom welcome to the Reverend Sam Ransom."

My face burned. My knees knocked. Vaguely, I remember the burst of applause and amens, the flurry of hands reaching out to pat me. What I do remember, the kind of unforgettable image on which a memory turns, were the two faces my eyes caught spinning from that blur of people.

At first, I wasn't sure. How long had it been, ten years, since Brown versus Board of Education, since our worlds parted? She was tall, dressed in white with her hair up, her skin lighter against the dominant black surrounding her. I whispered to myself, "God, can it be?" Then I saw that smile and a hand against her chest trilling a familiar shy wave. Beside her, lean and slightly shorter, was a young black male. The brightness of the high-hanging lights drawing them out, the pink burn scars. Goatee, afro hair and all.

I knew it was him.

5

The very first time I saw Early Holly, I was sitting in my window in my home watching him shimmy up a mimosa tree, dive onto honeysuckle vines draping the fence that ran beneath the tree then bounce off the vines onto the ground, squirt back up the tree and do it all over again, over and over. He was short and skinny, like me. He looked my age, but he was not my color.

I sat there watching him. He'd invented a game he could play against himself just to see how long he'd last, a thought that now seems prophetic. For the longest, I sat in my window until I couldn't stand to watch any longer and made a bee line out the backdoor.

He had a scrawny tube of neck, and his collarbones protruded sharply through an oversized T-shirt that was yellowish-gray around the bottom where he'd blown and wiped his nose. His blue jeans were too short, frayed at the knees and along the cuffs, and he used a rope for a belt. Pink, wrinkled blotches covered his arms and part of his face, as if someone had taken a hot steam iron and rubbed the skin the wrong way, burning off the brown.

He seemed not to notice me as I stood watching him shimmy up the mimosa tree again. He looked like someone climbing a telephone pole, his little pink soles and toes hooking onto the sides of the tree trunk. Uninvited, I stepped up and tried and slid to the ground. He bounced off the honeysuckle, circled again, and saw me but said nothing. I watched him go up the tree and I tried again, this time making it halfway up the trunk.

A long time that afternoon we played, crawling onto the limbs of the tree and swinging down onto the thick honeysuckle. For an eternity it seemed, we enjoyed our own version of catch-me-if-you-can, up the tree and onto the vines until he finally threw himself onto the ground and said, "I give." Looking back, I've often thought about those words, the first spoken between us, and their ominous import. I just showed up and inserted myself into his rhythm and we played in silence, the game and its rules materializing spontaneously, as most good things in life do.

Then he said again, "I give," and we lay under the tree and talked. We asked each other questions, the kind children ask upon first encounter. I told him I was eight years old and he said he was seven. He was in the second grade and went to the colored school across town, a long way from our block and his house. I was in the third grade and went to the elementary school just up the street. Then I asked a question that unraveled his story.

"My name is Sammy. What's yours?

"Early."

"How come you're called Early?"

"My mama, she was pickin' cotton and borned me in the cotton patch. Says they couldn't call me Cotton so they called me Early, 'cause I didn't come on time, she said. I been Early ever since."

"What's your daddy do?" I probed further.

His big brown eyes turned toward the ground and looked into the grass. "He's dead."

"How'd he die?" I asked, looking at the grass, too.

"The fire. Our house burned plum up. My mama said he run indoors to get me and thowed me through the winder. I only got burned some. But the fire, it got him and everthing." Big tears ran through the dirt on his face and dropped into the clover.

I reached over and patted him on the shoulder. "There, there. He's in heaven with my granddaddy. They're with God." For a while, my hand stayed on his shoulder. Beneath that mimosa tree, its wide umbrella branches arching over us, we lay quietly on our backs. White clouds floated above the treetops. Mockingbirds sang, and blue jays squawked at each other in the high limbs. The air was sweet with the smell of honeysuckle and clover.

I pointed out to him the house where I lived and the window where I'd been watching him. He hooked a thumb over his shoulder at a beauty parlor and said he lived there. I told him my father was a watchmaker, and my parents owned a jewelry store. He said his mother owned the beauty parlor and ironed women's hair. We spent the rest of the afternoon playing together, inventing one game after another that could be played with a tree, a fence and a thick honeysuckle vine until I heard my mother's whistle that it was dinnertime, and I had to go. We'd do it again we agreed, but set no appointed time. We didn't shake hands. High-fives hadn't come along. In all our rambunctious energy that afternoon, except for the moment I laid my hand on his shoulder, we never touched.

I went home that day smelling of honeysuckle. My mother looked at me when I came in and sniffed, but said nothing. That evening at the supper table the adult conversation quickly worked its way around to, "Sammy, what did you do today?" My father asked the question. My mother was looking down, moving her fork through a mound of black-eyed peas.

"I found a new friend," I said.

At the time, I had no idea the stir those five words would cause. I thought I understood my parents' opinions and feelings about colored people. I knew each spring, before Easter, my father went down to Taylor's Men's Store and bought Wes Schooler, a deranged town mascot of sorts, a pair of wingtip shoes and a new suit, complete with a silk tie and silk handkerchief for his coat pocket. I knew my father had saved our black gardener David Wade's life and paid the hospital bill. I knew poor folks, white or colored, would pick up their fixed watches and my father would say, "No charge." I knew my mother belonged to the Women's Society of Christian Service and would come home from their meetings telling my father that Negroes were children of God just like us. I thought I had found a new friend.

"Oh! Who's your new friend?" my father said calmly, raising a fork full of peas to his mouth.

"His name is Early. He lives at the beauty parlor across the street from Lula." Lula was our colored maid.

I don't recall feeling I'd done anything wrong, though my father's look suggested otherwise. His mouth clamped down on the black-eyed peas and he swung that same intense look, like it might have been a door slamming, on my mother. My mother's chin stiffened, and she gave my father a hard squint-eyed tight-lipped look. I thought maybe something was wrong with the black-eyed peas he'd just shoved into his mouth, but they tasted fine to me. I wondered if my mother had run Lula off again.

I wondered what else might be wrong. I wanted to say more about jumping from the tree onto the honeysuckle vines, how much fun that was, but I decided not to. I'd already said something that was wrong, though it seemed right, and saying nothing seemed safer than saying something. My mother must have felt the same way. That was the tense silence we ate in the rest of the evening. I finally decided to quit wondering and eat so I could leave and go to my room. I could feel nothing but mad around that table that evening, and somehow I was in the middle of it.

All because I had found a new friend.

Later, that evening in my upstairs room, I caught bits and pieces of the fight below and thanked the Lord I had a room above it. I heard Early's name and the word colored. I heard my father say, "Our own kind" and my mother say, "They're only children." I heard the words "They" and "We" a lot; "They" this and "We" that, like "They" and "We" were teams on opposite sides.

For a while, I didn't hear anything and thought the fight was over. Then my father said something, but all I could make out was the last word: "restrict." I didn't know what "restrict" meant, but my mother said the block was my world, that I shouldn't be restricted simply because I'd made a new friend. She sounded like she was on my side, if I had a side. She sounded like Early was a child of God, just like me.

At one point, I was beginning to connect pieces and put them together, and then all of a sudden, they started fighting about something else. My mother must have quoted scripture, something she was fond of doing, especially in arguments. My father told her she was taking her church too seriously, and my mother told him it was his church, too, and he wasn't taking it seriously enough. That started them off on something that had nothing to do with me.

That was a long night with long silences in between the long spell of loud voices. I'd hear the same broken fragments again and again, and after a while some semblance of understanding began to fall into place. I wasn't sure of all the reasons. I am fairly sure my father did not know all the reasons either. Despite all I had seen him do for colored people, what I didn't know was, in his mind, I had crossed a line I didn't see. My mother saw the line, but she thought it was all right for me to cross it.

I decided my mother won. No one told me I couldn't play with Early again.

Not then, anyway.

I turned off my light that night, looked out my window and beneath a full moon saw a lighted window where Early lived. I guessed the front part of the house was the beauty parlor, and he and his mother lived in the back because the lighted window was there. I wondered if Early's playing with me had stirred up as much in his house for having found a new friend as it had in mine. I wondered if his daddy, if he were alive, would have felt the same as mine. I wondered if his mother was like mine. I wondered if women were more understanding than men in these matters. I wondered how it was all going to turn out. I wondered till I could wonder no more and then said my prayers.

* * *

That mimosa tree and honeysuckle event took place in the spring of 1951. By summer, the first true summer of my life, Early and I were inseparable. We'd worn out the honeysuckle vine and turned to other pastimes. We wove clover chains, tied strings to June bugs and spun them through the air. We jumped and danced in the street cleaner's cool spray and clipped playing cards to our bicycle spokes with clothespins and rode them sputtering down the street sounding like motorbikes. In the evenings, we caught lightening bugs and put them in Mason jars, crickets in shoeboxes and frogs in cigar boxes, the world of nature in the palms of our hands.

My fenced-in palisaded backyard became a fort where we played long hours of cowboys and Indians that, one day, spawned an idea. I decided we needed to be more than friends. I'd seen a western about a cowboy and an

Indian. I'd slipped a razor from my father's Gillette package, one of many he wouldn't miss. Early and I sat in a ditch beside the beauty parlor in the shadows of a privet hedge and made small slits across our thumbs, winks of pain, then lay there, our thumbs pressed together, our hearts beating wildly, unaware that a line faraway in another state was being crossed.

In retrospect, I know the story well. Then, all I knew, from the news on radio, was that a colored third grader named Linda Brown, who lived somewhere in Kansas, had to walk one mile through a railroad switchyard to get to her elementary school even though a white elementary school was only a few blocks away. I thought of Early who had to walk just as far. Linda Brown's father tried to enroll her in the white school and was turned down.

Brown v. Board of Education is familiar to all of us now. The case ended up in the Supreme Court. Chief Justice Warren Burger read the unanimous decision of the court, a decision that forever changed my life and the lives of every southerner, black and white.

On May 17, 1954, Brown v. Board of Education hit my world.

I never rode again in the wagon with Giles.

I'd see him occasionally, usually around town when I was riding with my parents or washing the windows of my parents' store. That wagon would come rattling down Bankhead Street and I'd stop what I was doing. He'd stop too and we'd wave. But that was all.

I saw Early from time to time, but we never played again. A word I'd heard before was responsible: restrict. I would see him at a distance from my bedroom window where I'd first glimpsed him. I'd be sitting at my desk studying or reading and watch him mount his bike and pedal circles in the street or shoot basketball at a naked hoop his mother had rigged on a tree near the beauty shop, the ground beneath it worn to a slick patina. He'd never look up to see if I was looking, but I bet he knew. Once I watched him, with the same agility I'd seen before, climb the mimosa tree. The honeysuckle vine was still there, but not as lush. I thought surely he'd look up, but he never did. I wondered then if the same message was being preached at his house.

A few years later, I met him at Jitney Jungle. I was going in and he was coming out holding a small sack of groceries. He spoke first.

"Hey, man, how you doin'?" he asked smiling, but the smile carried no warmth.

"Fine, how about you?" I said returning the smile.

"Your mama's got you shopping, too?" he said.

Awkwardly, we stood there amid the traffic passing through the door, struggling for words that in other days came as easily as breathing.

"I'm in the tenth grade," I said. "You were a grade behind me."

"Yep, I'm in the ninth."

We didn't ask each other which schools. We knew those answers.

"How's your mama?" I said. I already knew because Lula kept me informed.

"Doin' mighty good. How 'bout yours?"

He probably knew that answer, too. Lula's caring spirit worked both sides of the fence. "She's fine," I said.

"Well, I gotta be going," Early said awkwardly. "See you around."

I said something similar and thought, as we departed, we might see each other sooner than expected. The year was 1957. Nine black students were barred from entering an all-white school in Little Rock, Arkansas, and President Eisenhower had used troops to force their entry. The government was taking a long time making Supreme Court decisions reality in Mississippi. But sooner or later, we'd be integrated and attending the same school.

* * *

In those days, sadly, another door closed.

Her name was Sharon Rose, a hybrid Southern double name, like Betty Sue, Jo Beth or Emmy Lou. Giles had introduced her as his niece that first summer day we met, but I thought then she was no more his niece than he was my uncle. Beside Giles, she looked almost white and beside me, tan: too light to be his color and too dark to be mine, somewhere in between but closer to mine than his. I wasn't sure what she was. Years later, when I asked my mother, she said she was probably a "light Negro," and that's all she would say.

I remember Sharon Rose said she was nine, the same age as Early that day we both met her when Giles stopped his wagon in front of my house. At the time, I felt no competition with Early, or jealousy, no resentment that another had suddenly joined our private duo. Early and I were glad to have a new friend, even if it was a girl.

Occasionally, Giles dropped off Sharon Rose to play with us, return on his way home and pick her up. My parents were always at work. Recalling the fight my first mention of Early caused, I said nothing to my parents about another new friend, though I suspected they knew. Neighbors gossiped, and we played all over the block. Maybe it was because they'd grown accustomed to seeing Early and me together and because Sharon looked almost white. Lula always knew when Giles dropped her off, and she didn't care as long as we stayed on the block within earshot. Lula was watching us even when we didn't know she was watching. We called Lula our "help," but she was much more. Lula could have taught a guardian angel a thing or two. Years later, I looked up the meaning of the name "Lula." I was not surprised: "Famous Warrior." She was every bit that.

The fact Sharon Rose was a different sex expanded the variations on our theme of play. Cowboys and Indians and Knights of the Round Table now had a damsel in distress. We had someone to rescue. We had an audience, someone to impress. Perhaps it began there, that special feeling for her.

I did not know why, but there were times I found myself wanting to get close enough to smell her, to touch her. I would choreograph games so I was the rescuer, the one who had to put his arm around her and whisk her from danger. Fall upon her to shield her from flying bullets. Hold her hand for her to follow me through dark jungles. Early went along and didn't complain. He was nearer her color, but he didn't seem to mind our closeness. Now, I realize he was simply accepting his place in the social and racial hierarchy of that time, one passed down from generation to generation.

I recall the last time I saw Sharon Rose, the last time our trio would be together in those halcyon summers we thought would never end. It was on a Saturday, the week before my twelfth birthday. Perhaps I knew, intuited, I would not see her again. Perhaps, the feeling was one I absorbed from

Lula and Giles, the grave expression that I saw more and more on their faces, an expression that said they saw something developing within our little triad that spelled trouble. Maybe they knew something we only sensed through them and the rest of our adult world, that a big change was coming and it wasn't going to be good. Perhaps that was why I stood with Early on the sidewalk in front of my house that late Saturday afternoon and waved to Sharon Rose with a sad heart as Giles snapped the reins, and the wagon began moving down the street.

I went to sleep that night cherishing hours of closeness I feared might never be again. Her hand in mine as I helped her down from the wagon when we stopped. The time Bud, Giles' mule, jolted, and she was thrown against me, her face on mine, her lips against my cheek, the dampness still there long after we parted. The serious look on her face when it happened, one that didn't say, "I'm sorry." Our legs touching as we sat across from each other in the bed of the wagon, our bare feet playing tag, "got you last." Early didn't seem to mind, at least not at first. He just scooted over and joined in.

In retrospect, those moments of physical touching were the first stirrings of sexual energy for me, something natural and of no great significance. They were memories that brought a smile, a private chuckle. Back then, those moments were cataclysmic. Strange, hard things happened to my body when we touched. During sleep, she'd be in my dreams and there were explosions, eruptions I couldn't explain but wanted to happen again and again. I waved with sadness that afternoon. I sensed something big leaving my life and leaving behind a great emptiness, one I would never fully understand. For months, she did not haunt me. I haunted her, conjured up her presence … everywhere.

Sharon Rose eventually drifted from my memory, or was eclipsed. I had my second girlfriend at age fifteen. Her name was Holly. She lived on our block, three houses behind mine. She was short, petite and dark-complexioned. I learned later that her mother was from Mexico. Her mother drove us to school each morning. We sat in the backseat. One thing led to another and we were holding hands. The same feelings Sharon Rose had sparked returned. I recalled those memories, but only briefly. Holly moved to Birmingham. I grieved but found a new love. I lost my virginity at age seventeen. And so it went, through high school and into college. At times, I wondered about the first love of my life, Sharon Rose. I have no memory of when the wondering stopped.

It just stopped.

6

Standing there against the back wall of that church that night, I could not believe I was seeing Sharon Rose Word and Early Holly and at a civil rights rally of all places. After my introduction, the meeting was soon over, and the two hastily threaded their way to the back where I stood waiting, unsure what else to do. We hugged and shared joys over seeing each other again. They needed to speak to others they said and asked me to wait outside.

Eventually, the crowd dispersed, and the lights in the church went out. Keys jangled, and the doors were locked. A lone figure walked to a car and drove away. At last away from everyone, we sat in my car. The humid night air was heavy. Except for the rise and fall of droning cicadas, it was still.

Early sat in the back seat. Physically, he'd not developed much differently than the last time I had seen him. He was taller but still skinny. The only differences were his bushy hairdo, which almost touched the roof of the car, and his goatee and sideburns that partially covered his burn scars but made his face look small. The scars always reminded me of his father's bravery and sacrifice. I have often imagined what it would be like to burn to death and recently read somewhere that many burned victims rarely feel the flames. By the time they reach them, they are already dead from smoke inhalation. There are some mercies in the laws of nature. I had no way of knowing then that Early had learned the incineration of their home and his father was not accidental. A white man's bigoted anger was behind it. But the man was never charged.

Sharon sat curled up, her back against the door on the front seat beside me. Her legs were tucked back, her knees round and slick in her pale silk hosiery. She still had the dainty nose and small chin I remembered. In a white blouse and skirt with large pearl earrings and white pumps, she looked lovely and elegant.

Her almond-shaped eyes brimmed with excitement, and they were on me. When she smiled, her teeth shone as white as the pearl earrings. The glow from a security light on the church grounds cast a silver edge to her features. There was no movement of wind, but the perfume she wore traveled in the humid air and seemed to take over the car. In a gesture of casual calmness, as though there'd been no gap in our friendship, she kicked off her heels and stretched out her legs then drew back her feet.

The two were as surprised as I by the sudden reunion. At first, we talked all at once, like excited friends on the first day of school reunited after a long summer's absence. We reminisced about the fun times we had had playing together as children. We laughed at some of the memories.

"Y'all remember when we were playing Knights of the Round Table," I said, "and, Early, you said you were tired of being the bad guy and you wanted to be a hero."

"Now you goin' to meddling," Early said in a pseudo scolding tone.

"I put my arm around you, Early," Sharon joined in with exaggerated sympathy, "and said 'you're not a bad guy. You are a hero, and we're just playing.'"

Smiling and entertained, Early said, "And I said I wanted to save you." He slapped Sharon playfully on her arm resting on the seat back.

She turned, reached over the backseat and popped him on the knee. "And you *have* saved me, many times," she said and winked at him.

"But you weren't going to let me be the Black Knight," Early said to me jokingly, his chin bobbing with easy laughter. "You said King Arthur's Round Table didn't have any black knights."

"You weren't to be outdone, Early," I reminded. "You said, 'He does now,' and you flashed your sword into the sky and shouted, 'Early the Black Knight.'"

Sharon looked at Early. "And you've been the Black Knight hence evermore, Hon." We all laughed at the remembrance of the episode and I sensed the playful affection, the warmth, between them.

I followed up with another memory. "Early, I've never forgotten the time we were playing cowboys and Indians, and you asked why there weren't any colored cowboys."

"And you couldn't answer the question," Early countered eagerly.

"No," I said, "but you did. You came to play one day all decked out, twirling your plastic pistols and jingling your spurs and proclaimed, "'I'm through bein' an injun. From now on, I'm a colored cowboy. Just call me C.C.'"

We laughed so hard and loud the clamor of cicadas outside subsided.

We told more stories of those memorable days. Then the adrenalin leveled out, and the mood turned quieter.

"Why are y'all here?" I said. "Sharon, I thought you were up North. And Early, I haven't seen you since when, seven, eight years ago?"

"About seven," he said. "We bumped into each other in town. You were coming out of Jitney Jungle. We didn't talk long."

I recalled the awkward incident and why so little was said. I looked at Sharon, at her dark eyes beneath the sickle-moon eyebrows.

"I did go up North," she said. "Elkhart, Indiana, to be exact. I lived there with an auntie for six years. There were problems at home, but that's a long story for another time." She turned her face toward the window briefly, then back. "I decided to return to Mississippi and go to Rust College. Actually, I got a scholarship, which helped the decision." She spoke almost without accent.

"Rust is in Holly Springs," I said. "How'd y'all get down here, to this place?"

"That's a long story, too," said Early. He and Sharon looked at each other and I saw again the chemistry I'd glimpsed earlier. "Sharon and I had a couple of classes together. We were getting close, so when I got a scholarship to Tougaloo in Jackson, she applied and got one too."

"Early's leaving out some things," she said. "We wanted to become involved in the Movement. There was pressure at Rust, that good ole Methodist school, not to rock the boat. The school might lose some of its funding from the good, white Methodists in the state. Sorry, Sammy, but it's true."

"I go by Sam now. And I know all about those good ole, white Methodists."

"We knew Tougaloo was a safe haven," she continued, speaking in soft rushes of passion. "Reverend King, the white minister who spoke tonight, is there and the Movement is alive and doing well there. That's why we are here. We volunteered to help rebuild the church down the road that was burned recently."

"Where are you staying?" I probed. "You can't be driving back and forth."

"Right now, we're staying with a family in Itta Bena," Sharon said. "It's in the Delta, not far from here."

"I know exactly where Itta Bena is," I said. "It's not far from Money, where Emmett Till was lynched."

There was a brief silence, as though in reverence, before Early leaned forward and wrapped his arms across the back of the seat. "Now it's your turn, Sam. Last we heard, you were in the big city of Atlanta."

"How'd you know that?"

"*New Albany Gazette*. There was an article about you," said Sharon. "My auntie read it and told me."

I gave them the short history, broad strokes and described the parish set up. The night was moving on, and I still had more questions for them. I asked about their school and studies. Sharon was studying to be a nurse. Early was in political science, hoping to become an attorney and champion civil rights. That certainly made sense. He'd once said he was going to be somebody.

*   *   *

I was ten years old. Early was nine and Mississippi was experiencing one of the hottest summers on record. The lemonade stand was my mother's idea, but Lula made the lemonade and cookies, and we sold them. Early had another idea and crafted a sign: LEMONADE, <u>ALL</u> YOU CAN DRINK, 10 cents. I told him we wouldn't make any money, but he pointed to one of the paper cups neatly arranged on the card table my mother had set up for us. "That is *all* you can drink." I can still see his face and eyes light up on *all*, that crescent smile minus two front teeth stretching his face.

We'd been sitting in small folding chairs beside the card table where our sign hung and where the pitcher and paper cups were displayed.

A man pulled up to the curb in a pickup truck. His arm was out the window and I could see the shiny dime already in his hand. Early saw it, too, and stepped forward to take it.

"I want some lemonade, but I ain't buying from no nigger," he said and made a fist around the dime just as Early reached for it.

Early said nothing and stepped back. I didn't know what to say. The man was our first customer. I walked up and took the dime and handed him a cup of lemonade. He gulped it down and handed me the cup back for another. "Sign says all you can drink for a dime."

Early spoke before I could respond. "That is *all* you get for a dime," he said.

"You smart ass nigger. I oughtta get out and whip your butt."

Lula opened the side kitchen door and came onto the porch. She stood there with her broom in her hand and glared at the man, and the man glared back at her. She didn't stop glaring at him and the man finally looked away. Early stepped back up onto the sidewalk.

"Here, you can have your dime back," I said, my knees knocking.

"Naw, you keep your goddamn dime. But you'd sell a lot more lemonade without the nigger."

He scratched off and sped up the street.

Lula stood there awhile longer. "You all right, Early?"

"Yessum." He pulled an arm across his eyes. "But someday I'm not gonna be a nigger. I won't ever be white like you," he said, scowling at me, "but I'm not gonna be a nigger. I'm gonna be somebody."

*   *   *

Leaning further across the car's seat back, as if to wedge himself more into the triad, Early made a comment about staging a sit-in protest, and the discussion took an interesting turn.

"There you go again, Early, pushing that direct action stuff," Sharon said turning around in the seat so she was facing him. "President Beittel wouldn't be leaving if it hadn't been for those sit-ins. All they do is rile the whites and cost us blacks in the long run."

"Who's Beittel?" I asked.

"Dr. Adam D. Beittel. He was the president at Tougaloo," Sharon said. "He was forced to resign."

"That's right, Shar," Early blurted back. "You folks just want to register voters and believe city hall will let 'em vote and that's going to bring change, and everything will be hunkydory. You know what happened in Laurel and Hattiesburg, not to mention Greenwood, Ruleville and McComb."

"Well, your SNCC crowd is going to cost us," Sharon countered, her pitch rising. "That's all I know. We ought to listen to Aaron Henry and Roy Wilkins. We've got so many groups down here now it's like alphabet soup—CORE, COFO, SNCC, SCLC. All we really need here are just some dedicated people helping other people, doesn't matter what color, to build their churches and teach them and their children to read so they can register to vote. If we get enough of our people voting, we can create change."

She was making more sense than the speakers I'd heard that night in the church.

Early leaned back in the seat and made a trailing comment. "Well, we start building tomorrow. Wanna join us, Sammy? I mean Sam."

I was still reflecting on my first glimpse of division within the black mindset. I would learn later of the serious rifts between the various factions within the state and nation, the rifts within the rifts. This information was firsthand from the players themselves and not the secondhand rhetoric I was used to hearing on a predominately white campus. It was an era of monoliths. Communism and Democracy. Black Power and White Supremacy. Doves and Hawks. Until you moved within the myths and discovered the people, the individuals. I felt Sharon had touched the essence. There were other reasons, too, why I leaned toward her position.

"I guess I'm just a quiet Christian who believes in helping others," I said and then added, "regardless of color. I asked Uncle Giles once what do preachers do, and he said, 'Do right and help others.'"

Early popped up again on the seat back and jumped on the comment. "He said that to me, too. So, if you want to make him proud, you'll help us?"

"It would be like old times," Sharon said. She leaned over and placed a hand on my arm and squeezed. Her eyes were close and large, her smile inviting. I thought a long moment before answering.

"It would be the right thing for me to do," I finally said.

"Great!" they exclaimed in unison.

"But it would be the wrong thing for the churches I am committed to serving."

"That's bullshit," Early shouted angrily.

"Early!" Sharon snapped raising an eyebrow of restraint.

"It's just a cop out," Early said harshly.

I could see the anger in his face and feel it in his voice, and I recalled the scowl that long ago afternoon when we were selling lemonade. *Someday I'm not gonna be a nigger.*

"He's got his congregations to think about," she said.

I was looking around at the vacant churchyard, thinking how vacant eleven others would be at preaching time if I helped rebuild a Negro church.

"Those congregations, as you put it," Early continued, his lips curled and his teeth and whites of his eyes flashing, "are the very people who are bombing and burning our churches and meeting places and cars and trying to keep us in submission."

"It's okay," I said. "I understand. I need for you to know how I feel," and looked straight at him. I was still stunned at his comment. "There is a part of me that says, 'Yes, go for it.' Then there's this other part that says, 'Take one step at a time,' and yet another that whispers loudly, 'No way. You'll get yourself killed.' I guess when you peel away the emotional layers and get down to the raw nerves, I just don't have your vision, which means I don't have the courage."

Early leaned further over the seat and got in my face. "You can't go on just the vision. You can't just see it. You have to be the vision. Maybe you don't have the courage 'cause it ain't your cause. You know what I mean.

It wadn't your people killed, beaten and driven from their homes. You know what I mean. It wadn't your people denied the right to vote and made to look like nincompoops when they did. You know what I mean. It wadn't your people—"

"Okay, Early, you've made your point," Sharon stopped him, her body beautifully twisted on the seat as she looked at him.

In the pressure of his speech, his grammar had slipped a notch, back to the sounds and syllables I remembered as a child when we rode with Giles and played together. "*You know what I mean*," he was saying, like I was supposed to be inside his skin. I had some understanding of what he meant, but what I knew was a knowledge that was not quite knowledge, one far above the emotional layers and raw nerves. I could see the sweat on his face and the wild excitement in his eyes. He had made his point and leaned back once more, brooding in the shadows of the backseat. I could feel the rebuff and wondered what had happened to that special bonding of our childhood. What had happened to our blood-brotherhood? I also sensed all was not well between him and Sharon. She was still glaring at him. I had sensed a genuine warmth between them, but something else was going on, something before I came on the scene.

"Maybe we should let Sam, *our friend*," Sharon said with emphasis, "take it one step at a time."

I will never know if, during the heat of discussion, she was aware of what had happened. Her feet had slipped further across the seat and her toes, tucked into the crease, were beneath me, barely touching my buttocks. I didn't move a muscle, afraid she'd shift and take them away. I recalled sitting in the wagon bed across from her, our bare feet playing tag. *Got you last.* I'd always wondered why it was "Got you last." Why not "Got you first?"

There was a long silence, then Sharon looked at her watch. "Guess we better be getting on," she said slipping her shoes back on.

I was disappointed but could think of nothing to say that might continue the evening except exchanging contact information. We agreed I could reach them where they were staying, and they could call me at the parsonage, but not the church.

"You never know who's going to answer the phone there," I said.

"Yeah," said Early, "one step at a time." His tone was sarcastic, but passed unchallenged.

I thought about friendship and what can happen to it, about what a handful of years of different ideas and beliefs can do to a relationship.

We looked around like paranoids before getting out of the car.

I followed them to their car, a green Ford station wagon, mid-fifties model. Early said the family they were staying with had let them borrow it. I had opened the passenger door for Sharon. Early told her to hurry and get in. Though it was a new moon, and the night darker than usual, perhaps he was concerned we were too visible there in the churchyard, two blacks and a white. I hugged Sharon. She put her arms around me and patted me on the back of the head.

"You take care, Sam Ransom," she whispered into my ear. "You hear?"

"You, too," I said, squeezed her once more, then watched her slide into the car.

I walked around the front of the car to hug Early, but he extended his hand, a signal he needed distance. I understood, and we shook. His grip was firm, too firm.

"Call us if you decide to take that step," Early said.

"I will. Count on it."

"I will. Count on it," he parroted ironically. His way of *got you last* I thought.

I watched until their taillights vanished in a boiling swirl of dust and the dark.

Driving back, I thought of Early and his afro look. When I reflect on that time, the images that come to mind are heroes of his color, of Julian Bond, Andrew Young and a young black from Illinois, who gave the keynote address at the last Democratic Convention, Barack Obama. Early was one of them. I felt he was truly going to be somebody.

Mostly, I thought of Sharon, how good she looked. It would be some years, 1983, before there would be a black Miss America, but Sharon Rose Word, on any given day, hands down, would have beaten Vanessa Williams. Sharon was that gorgeous, and that confident, not the shy pigtailed girl of my youth. I wondered what she thought of me, if I'd come as far as she. Probably not. She'd traveled a road and distance I would never travel, that other story for another time. Not even if she told me her story blow-by-painful-blow would I fathom that journey's meaning for her, much less for me. That was the look I caught on her face before she turned and looked out the window, as if to avoid pain, a slap maybe, coming from the other side. By the standards of my culture, I should have felt above her. Instead, I felt beside her, with her ... for her. Already, I missed her. If she were white and I black, I'd be lynched for what I was thinking, one more body washed up years later on some lake shore or creek bank. If my thoughts were broadcast among my own, they would save the rope, waste no time with hanging, and invest a bullet. All the more reason I needed to be vigilant and careful about what I said. I did not think my thoughts were wrong. I did not feel guilty. I was skating on ice I thought thick as a concrete slab.

I did think I had found a new friend.

I wanted to see her again.

I drove on through the night with the windows down, my arm hanging cockily over the side. In those moments, I was fearless, delightfully and dangerously alive and had no second thoughts and felt no apprehension until I was near the first intersection north of Acona and noticed headlights behind me. Orange through the trailing dust, they were at a distance. I turned off gravel onto macadam, headed north toward Blackhawk and slowed to check the rearview.

The lights turned with me.

I speeded up.

They stayed with me.

At Blackhawk, I turned east onto the state highway. The lights were still there. They followed me to the Mount Pleasant city limits, then vanished.

7

Thursday, July 9

The next day began uneventfully. I drove to Greenwood in the Delta to visit several parishioners in the hospital and stopped at Waverley on my way back to check in briefly with Brother Allshouse. I told him how receptive my congregations had been and that my summer was going well. He said he was not surprised and passed on favorable comments he had heard. I said nothing about my experience the previous evening. Afterwards, I made several calls in the Redbone area. Though I did not travel the same roads I did the night before, I crossed them and each time thought again of my old friends, especially of Sharon Rose. The image of her curled up in the front seat was one I couldn't shake.

My biggest dilemma was finding a way, in broad Mississippi daylight, to help rebuild a burned Negro church. I'd have to pull off a magician's act, create an illusion of visibility, of busyness on my circuit and invisibility while working at the Negro church. I reasoned I could visit parishioners in the evenings. No one was monitoring my work. I could always blame my absence on the large charge. I did have to answer to Brother Allshouse and, ultimately, to Brother Hammingtree, the District Superintendent. But no one was looking over my shoulder or clocking my time. Several ideas came to mind, most of them weak.

One o'clock. Back at the parsonage, I slapped together a bologna sandwich and guzzled a glass of milk. I spent the afternoon visiting at Mars

Hill and Mount Pleasant. My stops were brief, but appreciated. I did the things I could do, was supposed to do—asked about family, read from the Bible, prayed. Sometimes I just sat in silence, my obligatory presence sufficient. Little things, I learned, go a long way. Visitation, I knew, was on that short list of requirements. Remembering names and keeping the parsonage lawn mowed were near the top.

I returned to the parsonage about six o'clock and ate another bologna sandwich and drank another tall glass of milk, with one addition to the menu. Mr. Dance had left a basket of fresh, vine-ripe tomatoes on the side doorstep.

The evening began quietly enough. I organized my books and papers on the living room floor to begin writing Sunday's sermon. Concentration was a struggle. I picked up the phone once to call Sharon but quickly returned the receiver to the hook. The call was probably long distance, but I'd pay the church back. Surely, no one would check the calls when they got the bill.

I thought Sharon might call, but she never did. I thought of Early's hostility and wondered again what had happened to our childhood camaraderie, those bonds of adventure and risk, imagined dangers and dramatic escapes. I recalled making clover chains, chasing the ice man and riding bicycles until we dropped. I thought of secret places and secret acts. I thought of our blood brother commitment. I thought of lazy summer days we lay on cushions of clover and gazed at the sky and solved our salvation beneath puzzles of clouds and the word "drift" came to mind. The winds of our cultures had blown us apart.

I lay in bed that evening unable to go to sleep, the solution to my predicament as elusive as ever. It seemed I would drift—that word again— without decision the rest of the summer.

I eventually fell asleep and a noise awakened me. I didn't own a radio, but the voices I heard sounded like voices from a radio turned low or from a distance, a nearby house perhaps. Many people left their windows up on summer nights, especially if they didn't have air conditioning. I'd left mine up because I wanted to hear the night sounds, the lulling monotony of cicadas, crickets and whippoorwills. Then again, maybe it was just men talking at Ivy Lee's gas station downtown two blocks away. They gathered there most nights late, sitting in cane bottom chairs and on upended Coke cartons, swapping stories and watching the cars go by. Sound does travel in a small town that has gone to bed.

Then I heard a loud *clank*, a hammer perhaps thrown into a pickup bed. Or tailgate slammed shut. It came from the front of the house. My bedroom was in the back. I slept in my jockey shorts, so I fumbled around in the dark for my blue jeans. The thought occurred to pick up the telephone, which was in the living room, and call for help. But the noises might be nothing, maybe someone fixing a flat. I got the top button of my blue jeans snapped and heard feet scuffling on the small porch around the front door. Then three loud reports, like gunfire.

I hit the floor facedown.

The feet on the porch scurried away. Someone had knocked on the door. That's all it was. Then, I smelled something strong, something with an edge to it: Kerosene.

My heart was a hammer finishing off the nails on the floor. My bones filled with lead. I couldn't get up. I lay breathing, waiting. There was a whoosh, sucking sound then an orange flare of reflected light. Through the bedroom door, I saw the living room light up. An engine roared and revved followed by squeals of rubber on concrete. I continued lying on the floor. The living room flickered with yellow light. The sound and smell of burning wood were distinct. I was certain I'd been firebombed and the front of the house was aflame, but I saw no smoke.

I was afraid to stand. What if they shot through the window? I crawled on my stomach into the living room where the phone sat on a doily on a small table. Still, no smoke. I could see the tips of flames dancing outside the front window. I pushed up slowly to peek and saw, engulfed in flames, a large cross.

I reached to pick up the phone and it rang. With a trembling hand, I lifted the receiver and brought it to my ear. "This here's just a reminder," a rough voice said. "Stay away from niggers and nigger lovers, or we'll burn more 'n a cross next time. You got that, preacher boy?"

The man hung up, but the voice lingered. The following Sunday, I would connect it with a hand I shook. I ate no more vine ripe tomatoes deposited on the side stoop. The honest look and smile on Mr. Dance Dorsey's face fit him like a Halloween mask.

I remained in the living room, lying low until the flames died. I thought of calling the police, then thought against it. They probably already knew. Many of them were in the Klan. I looked at my watch. Almost two thirty.

I waited a long time until the usual sounds of night returned and all seemed normal before I cracked the front door and peeked out. The cross was a smoking stake, its crosspiece dangling askew. I opened the door wider, stepped onto the small porch and surveyed the neighborhood. No lighted windows, no passing cars. My watch said almost three. The sun would rise between five and six. That was the last thing I needed, neighbors walking out to get their morning papers and seeing a burned cross in the front yard of the parsonage.

I located an old garden hose covered with leaves at the side of the house, hooked it up and doused the charred remains. I found a pile of rags in the garage closet and wrapped them around the cross's blackened base. It pulled easily from the ground, and I dragged it behind the garage. The crosspiece had burned considerably and broke easily. In the high grass, the two pieces would be hard to see, reminding me that the yard needed mowing.

I lay awake the rest of the night listening to the metallic and relentless grind of the cicadas, analyzing every noise, wondering what I should do. The sun barely up, I made the phone call I dreaded but knew I had to make, then dressed and got into the car.

8

Friday, July 10

Brother Allshouse was waiting for me when I arrived at his parsonage. Mrs. Allshouse opened the door and ushered me into his small study. She was solemn, rigidly cordial and departed immediately.

"Sit down!" he said briskly. He was sitting behind his desk leaning forward, a constricted, sullen look on his face.

I took the same rocker I'd taken previously directly across from him.

"Now, I will make this brief and to the point," he said casting a sharp critical look at me. "What in the name of God Almighty could have caused the Klan to burn a cross in the front yard of the Mount Pleasant parsonage, pray tell?" His glasses slid down his nose and he pushed them back into the notch that bridged his thick brows. He raised himself in his chair, twitched his shoulders like an animal vexed by a fly and leveraged his voice an octave. "Pray tell."

Those were the words of the moment, declarative and in that order. Pray and tell. After a millisecond prayer I cleared my throat. I was afraid to look at him, so I picked a spot on the window behind him, to the right of his hairline.

"I went to one of the meetings."

His fingers had been drumming soundlessly on the edge of the desk then stopped. His eyes rolled. "You went to one of the meetings," he whispered sarcastically.

"Yes sir."

He leaned back. His fingers drumming again. "Go ahead," he said rolling a hand. "There's more to this."

I told him about the meeting at the church with Brodsky and Rubin. I explained that there were fellow ministers involved from other parts of the country, maybe even Methodists, a long way from home. They were brothers of the faith and needed a show of support. The least I could do was offer some moral support. I was not one of them, I emphasized, merely an invited guest. This was still the United States of America, land of the free, and I should be allowed to visit the church of my choice. I didn't stop there. I brought to bear an incident remembered by some, forgotten by many.

"In January of last year," I said, "twenty-eight Mississippi Methodist ministers, born of conviction, signed a declaration condemning discrimination because of race, color or creed."

He nodded, almost imperceptibly.

I continued. "That took courage. I don't know if I would have signed the document had I known about it. But I do believe this. I can't see Jesus standing in the door of a church saying, 'Now, you there, John and Charles and Susan, y'all come on in, but you over yonder, Leroy and Luke and Clytee, you can't come in because you're colored.'"

He nodded again and waved a flippant hand in the air. "Yes, yes. I know all that," the tone of his voice softer. "But did you know those ministers, one by one, began leaving the state?"

"I did not," I had to admit.

"As for Jesus," he said. "If he'd had a family, he might have stayed away from Jerusalem. His family might have come before a cause. A cause is an idea. A family is flesh and blood."

I couldn't believe my ears. He'd left himself wide open. I lunged. To make it all the more poignant, I stood up and leaned over the desk. "The word became flesh."

"So?" he said, his hands knitted across his paunch, a smug what's-the-point look on his face.

Symptomatic of the culture that produced him, and me, he'd obviously failed to connect the dots. In one of those rarefied "finest moments" we all have and never forget, I would do it for him. "God put his family, his only family, his only son, on the line."

It was a *tour de force*. Embarrassment climbed his neck into his balding scalp. He gave a gruff "hump" and looked at the top of his desk. A long silence followed. I didn't sit back down because I sensed our meeting was over. He stood and nervously hitched his pants with his elbows.

"Well, I was just trying to protect you." Then he said, "Do what you feel *you* need to do on your own," he continued, "but don't offer the church's services to them. And mind you, the nightriders mean business. Their theology is skin deep, if that. It could be *more* than a cross burning next time."

I knew the response, but thought I should ask. "Do you think I should report this?"

"Naw. Law enforcement already knows. The authorities around here *are* the Klan. That'll just make 'em think you're scared. I'd leave it alone."

I let myself out of his home. Driving back to Mount Pleasant, I thought about his remarks. I was single, had no family. I had no house payment, no rent to pay. I *was* in a position to throw my life for something. Before, the Movement had been just an idea. Then it turned personal.

A cross had been burned in *my* yard.

9

I was naive enough to think the incident, because it happened in the pitch of night with the world dead asleep, would never see the light of day. But by Friday noon, upon my return from my meeting with Brother Allshouse, the entire town was abuzz. The telephone at the parsonage was ringing when I opened the door. It was Dot Foster, chairwoman of the parsonage committee. She was frantic and wanted to know the state of the parsonage. She had heard the Klan had thrown a bomb at it.

Next, Lloyd Kistner called. He was one of the stewards and owned the hardware store in town. Ivy Lee at the service station had told him the parsonage had been firebombed. Others called, all members of the Mount Pleasant church. Their first questions were about the parsonage, my safety an afterthought, it seemed, in their assigned priority of values. I assured each the parsonage was intact and had not been firebombed. The only damage done, a burned circle in the lawn. They seemed satisfied and queried no further. The damage control was working and would hold, I thought. I began to relax.

I washed down a peanut butter and jelly sandwich with a half glass of milk and left. The folks east of town in Lebanon, Beulah Grove and Mars Hill surely hadn't had time to hear the news. Redbone to the west, maybe. For some reason, I sensed the wind blowing from that direction. I headed east, convincing myself I was ahead of the gossip front.

Silas Cash was a Beulah Grove member. His small store was at the intersection of two gravel roads. On busy days, while crisscrossing the county, I would stop there several times. Across the front, a large homemade sign said CASH'S GROCERY. Its paintless and weathered boards were checkered with tobacco and snuff and soft-drink signs—Bull of the Woods, Days Work, Grapette. They patched the windows and door. A single gas pump stood in front, the old-fashioned type that looks like a rocket with a glass nose. On each side of the entrance were crude wooden benches. Sitting on them that afternoon were men from that neck of the woods. Men wearing overalls and brogans and wide straw hats. Men talking and whittling and spitting, rolling cigarettes. Slouch-shouldered they sat, eyes on the ground but seeing everything going on around them. The type that sat around all day, but had plenty to do at night. Men stirring up dark inventions. I thought of another store. Another time. Other men.

* * *

Giles pulled the wagon into line at the sawmill. Two wagons were ahead of us, which meant time for a cold drink and a candy bar at Gravlee's, a store near the sawmill.

Gravlee's was overrunning with people, country folk and farmers. The benches in front were full. A few Negroes gathered around a small tree near the store. I stayed close to Giles as we walked toward the store. He motioned me to stay outside. I found an empty drink carton and carried it to a spot not far from the small tree and closer to the street.

I was minding my own business sitting on the carton watching traffic. I looked up and a cold chill went through me. My insides shook. The Ruthven brothers were across the street staring and pointing at me.

The summer before, Early and I had been shooting marbles on the sidewalk in front of my house when I felt eyes on us and heard someone breathing behind me. Whoever it was had been there awhile, waiting. I turned and looked. An ugly face covered with red pimples was grinning down at me.

"Well, if it ain't the four-eyed, nigger-loving bastard," the face said.

I jumped up and slapped his pimpled face. Early ran one way toward the side street and I rushed onto the porch and into the house, crying, "Lula, Lula." I cried all afternoon. Lula held me and tried to comfort me. She kept asking me what was wrong, and I could only tell her a bad person called me a bad name and I slapped him. She asked me what the name was, but I didn't want to say it. Uncle Giles had told me once never to say that word.

I had nightmares for weeks, saw my body beaten and mangled in the city dump. Except for trips with Giles, I was afraid to leave the house alone. When I did, I was constantly looking over my shoulder. I told Giles about what had happened and he said, "Remember, Chile. You is what you is. What somebody calls you don't make you what you is."

They were coming toward me, their eyes glaring. Their faces looked mean. They crossed the street, shirttails flapping, thumbs hooked in the belt loops of their pants. They walked through the traffic like bad men in a western swaggering through a crowded saloon. Tires screeched. Horns honked.

My insides shook more. I was afraid to look up and kept my eyes down. I felt sick to my stomach.

The sounds of their boot-heel taps left the street and clumped on hard clay. They were coming closer. I couldn't tell their footsteps from my pounding heart. The ground where I was looking suddenly became shadow.

The shadow shouted, "Well, if it ain't the four-eyed, nigger-lovin' bastard." It was Eugene, the biggest of the three.

Everyone around Gravlee's heard it. Talking stopped. The only sounds were the buzz of the sawmill blades and the clanging of the blacksmith's hammer.

I still didn't look up.

A boot from the shadow kicked the ground. Red clay peppered my legs. Dust boiled up into my face. Blood pounded in my temples. I broke out in a sweat. I felt like crying, but didn't dare.

I finally raised my head, tilted it back. Beneath the bill of my cap, the sun was blinding over the shoulder of the big Ruthven standing over me.

"Maybe he cain't hear with them goggles on," Eugene said.

The other two cackled.

"Sic 'im, Eugene," one said.

"I says, four-eyed—"

"He hears you," a familiar voice called from the store.

I looked to my left and saw Giles walking toward me.

"You be's mighty brave picking on somebody half yo' size," Giles said to Eugene. "And bringin' two mo' to help." One hand hung straight at his side; the other patted his belt buckle, the one he'd told me he wore in the war.

People circled, moved closer.

"Sit down, ole nigger man. This here ain't got a ga'damn thing to do with you," Eugene blurted.

"'Fraid so, lessen' there's another culud man here you callin' nigger. Sammy, you move right here behind me," Giles commanded, the hand hanging down his side pointing, the other still patting his buckle.

I couldn't move.

"Sammy, git yoreself up 'fore I kick that ga'damn drink box straight up yore ass," Eugene said. "Cain't hide in yore fancy house this time. I'm gonna stomp shit outta you, you little nigger-loving bastard."

Suddenly, from behind me, a swishing, slapping noise. Then a whirring sound, like someone whirling a rock on the end of a string. Giles stepped between me and Eugene. He was breathing fast and swinging his belt over his head like a lasso. The big brass buckle was whistling, flashing in the sunlight. barely missing Eugene's face.

Eugene began ducking and cussing. Giles took a step, Eugene hopped back. Giles took another step, Eugene hopped again, screeching in a loud whine, his face white as high noon, "Ain't none o' you white men gonna stop this ga'damn nigger?"

No one in the crowd moved.

Giles had Eugene hopping all the way back to where his brothers were standing. "Move on, younguns, befo' you cut to bacon strips," Giles said, looking right at them, swinging the buckle close to their faces.

All three were ducking, cussing and hopping like animals, back to the edge of the onlookers. Giles took one step closer and the Ruthvens turned and ran through the crowd, bumping and knocking people over. They reached the clearing before the river and kept going, disappearing down the bank.

I was never bothered by Eugene or any Ruthven again. What happened became the talk of the town. Before word could reach my parents, Giles walked with me to the store and told them. My parents were deeply appreciative and my father, for the first time, seemed to warm to Giles.

* * *

I opened the door and got out of the car. None of the men on the benches at Cash's Grocery looked up.

Not a one.

I said, "Howdy, y'all," as I crossed the plane of the awning's shadow. There were inaudible mumbles, but no head raised to acknowledge my salutation or presence as I passed on between the two benches and opened the screen door. Inside, an overhead fan moved hot air around. Mr. Cash wore a bloodstained butcher's apron and stood in his usual spot behind the U-shaped counter. He was talking with two older women looking over a stack of plaid shirts on a side counter. Several older men, regulars I had seen there before, were playing dominos in the back. The screen door had a stretched spring and was slow shutting. Mr. Cash turned and noticed me. His greeting was civil—faint smile and flat, "Hidy, Brother Sam, how you?"—minus his usual, cheery, "Preacher, come on in the house."

Before I could respond, the women, their small talk jarred by my entry, dropped the shirts they were examining. The dominos in the back stopped clicking. I returned Mr. Cash's hello and headed for the drink box under the front window, its chilled condensation the only relief in sight. Through dust-coated panes, I could see the men outside. They were still hunched over, their eyes still on the ground. I studied their backs and wondered if they knew I was looking. I knew none of them. Or did I? Was that why they wouldn't look up, their eyes driving their dark guilt into the dust.

I raised the large lid of the drink box, pulled out a Coke dripping with icy water, then lowered the lid. The bottle felt good in my hand, and I hoped the cool would spread. I popped the cap on the side opener and walked back to the counter and laid a quarter on its cracked linoleum top. Mr. Cash raised up from some work beneath the counter that had suddenly beckoned him. He took the quarter and said nothing as he rang up the sale, dropped the coin into the cash register, then ducked again beneath the counter. He rummaged and stirred around as though he were moving inventory.

I took a few swigs from the Coke. The ladies had resumed murmuring about shirts. Dominos commenced slapping and clicking in the back. It was as though a gust of uncertain wind had swept through the small building and taken away whatever distraction had briefly circulated.

I finished my Coke, guzzled it down and left with a friendly good-bye to Mr. Cash. He mumbled something unintelligible but he never raised up. Something Jesus had said about shaking the dust off your feet came to mind. I thought the screen door would slam on my way out, but the sprung spring closed it gently with a soft slap, like the eyes on my back following me to the car.

They would go inside when I left.

They would talk.

At each stop I made the rest of the day, the reception was cool and distant. Loose handshakes. Averted eyes. Short sentences. Nothing to prolong discussion. Nothing to encourage me to sit a spell in a rocker and sample a freshly baked pie or walk to a back pasture to check on cows. No one mentioned the incident.

I didn't know how they knew.

But they knew.

10

Sunday, July 12

I had to face my congregations. I'd spent the night before thinking about the sermon, thinking about what Giles might preach, what scripture he would choose. I knew one thing. Whatever topic he chose, he wouldn't back down from his convictions.

"If a man says he loves God and hates his brother, he is a liar." I pondered that scripture from Saint John's first letter. They were the right words for the right time. I thought of possible consequences. None could be worse than rustic chatter about a cross burning. I picked up my pen and began writing.

I preached five times that Sunday, starting at eight o'clock in the morning and finishing up at Redbone at six o'clock that evening. For a hot July in small clapboard churches, in a smothering suffocating heat, the services went smoother than expected. Hymns were sung. Prayers said. Babies cried. Wasps circled and made parabolic dives from the ceiling. Women batted the stifling air back and forth with cardboard funeral fans. Rigorously, and with feeling, I preached a fifteen-minute sermon. "In Christ There Is No East Or West" was the closing hymn. The benediction was something new I'd tailored to the message: "Go now and may the love of God erase all hate. In the name of the Father, the Son, and the Holy Spirit. Amen."

At each church, people departed faster than usual. A few stopped at the door, shook my hand and offered comments.

A "sweet sermon on love," said one lady.

"Lovely message on love," said another.

"Too bad none of them radicals weren't here today to hear it," one man stated emphatically.

All said they enjoyed the sermon.

Sadly, no one heard it.

Except at Redbone.

"You told me you wadn't no libr'al, but I hear'd you was at that church where all them com'inists meet," said Mr. Hunsucker. He raised his brows. "That right?"

A short thick finger was pointing at me like a pistol barrel. He had come from behind and stopped me just as I'd reached my car to leave. The question caught me off guard. I didn't think about my response, it just came out. "Mr. Hunsucker, the first time we met you asked me if I was liberal. Now you're asking me if I'm a communist. You have yet to ask me if I'm a Christian."

He scratched his face with the hand that had been pointing at me, looked down then back up at me, his narrowed eyes seeming to soften. "Well sir, you're a preacher right enough. But … it's hard to tell now days. Some folks'll run with the rabbits and hunt with the dogs."

I held back a smile at the line that should've been mine. "Rest assured, Mr. Hunsucker. I'm a Christian. I'm not a communist."

He made a silly little blink, gave me a half look, and turned away. But the carriage of his back as he walked away, his neck sucked into his shoulder blades, had a serious and ponderous sway.

*   *   *

Mississippi mid-summer is like an oven that bakes during the day, leaks heat at night and never cools down. The moon—full, half or quarter—blazes like a small sun, and the electric buzz of the cicadas saws the heavy, heat-laden air. Afternoon clouds carry a hope of rain that seldom brings relief. When it does rain, the downpour is brief and afterwards the air boils upward from the ground. Humid breezes at night only move the heat around, stopping now and then for the dust to settle in different places.

That Sunday night after the services, I lay in the midst of that heat on damp sheets that stuck to me. I looked through the window and the braided oak boughs into an infinite sky and listened to the languid trill of whippoorwills. Instead of *whip poor will, whip poor will*, as my grandfather had said they were saying, all I could hear was *whip poor Sam, whip poor Sam*. I lay there a long time … and thought.

The services had gone smoothly enough. But as carefully crafted, sharply honed as it was, the sermon had no edge. No one's thinking was penetrated. Except Hunsucker's. He got it.

I thought of the cross burning, the encounter with Mr. Hunsucker and Brother Allshouse's haunting words: *The nightriders mean business … it could be more than a cross burning next time.* I lay still as I could and listened for unnatural noises of the night. I thought of a firebomb hurled through the front living room window and me in the back bedroom unable to escape in time. I imagined my car torched under the carport, the explosion blowing the house into the trees. The Klan had been known to kidnap people in the middle of the night, tie their hands and feet, throw them into a river or a pond, then stand around, drink beer and watch.

Those were the horrors, the fears, that visited me in those desperate days.

I reflected on an evening the first week I had arrived. I had gone raccoon hunting with Red Kilmichael. We sat on a moss-covered stump and talked while the dogs ran. We listened to their changing yelps above the night insects, occasional hoots of an owl and howls of a coyote. We'd arrived at a tree where a coon was hugging the thin bole at the top, its eyes burning with fright in the glare of our flashlights. Mr. Red had just remarked how pitiful they looked, like a tiny person before execution.

I had been waiting for the opportunity. "Mr. Red, what do you think happened to those three fellows, the civil rights workers down in Philadelphia?"

I couldn't see the look on his face in the dark, but his shadow was rigid. His head never turned as he spoke. "Can't say as I know. But it don't sound good."

"Would that ever happen up here?"

"Could."

In the long silence, I studied his motionless, craggy silhouette and waited for him to say more. He looked back up at the scared coon and turned out the flashlight.

I never raised the subject again, but his earlier comment about defenseless creatures haunted me. That was the cloudless night, too, when we noticed the full moon was no longer full but quartered. Then halved.

I was speechless.

"The eclipse," Mr. Red said. "They said in the news it would be tonight, June twenty-five. A total eclipse."

We watched as the shadow continued to crawl until there was only a shaving of light … then nothing. Everything was blanketed with the sudden dark and I felt the silent weight of the night as all sound stopped, as if the nocturnal creatures, too, were engulfed in this strange march of the unseen sun. Then a thin arc of light appeared again. And again, as if on cue, the wood sounds of the night started up.

I thought about Eli Rubin's remark at the church, one that would hang permanently in my memory. Risk *was* what it was all about. It was a Jew who said those words to me, and my mind ripped back through two thousand years of history to another Jew who said the same thing. "Greater love hath no man than this, that he lay down his life for his friends."

When I look for guidance in making decisions, I tend to find myself in the small town where I was raised. Most of the defining moments in my life seemed to go back to that time riding in the wagon with Giles and listening. *Back down from the truth, and you livin' the lie.*

One more time, Uncle Giles, wherever you are, thank you.

Lying there that night, reflecting on Giles' wisdom, I wondered at what moment would I truly trust my feelings, my convictions? At what point was the true and still center of my being defined? I didn't have an answer, but I recalled a quote from C. S. Lewis, something I'd jotted down and had used once in a sermon: "Courage is not simply one of the virtues, but the form of every virtue at the highest testing point, which means at the highest point of reality."

I sensed that testing point was still ahead of me.

Overnight, those thoughts grew in my head. I woke up the next morning and thought of nothing else.

PART II

11

Monday, July 13

"She ain't in," said the aged voice over the phone. "Her and the other man out doing somethin'. 'Spect 'em back sometime this mornin'."

I called again at eleven o'clock. Same message. They were probably out canvassing or at the church. I tried again around noon.

"Hello, Sam Ransom," Sharon answered, her voice a little raspy, like the beginning of a cold. "We've been wondering about you. Haven't heard a peep."

"The silence has been me in deep thought."

"We know that kind of silence."

"I've decided to help you build the church," I said.

For a moment, all I heard on the other end was a deep breath then, "Praise God. Oh, that's such good news. Early'll be tickled. When are you joining us?"

"Tomorrow too soon?"

"Not a minute. Can we help?"

"My car's marked by the Klan."

"We've already solved that one," she said, that confident tone in her voice I recalled from the night we reunited.

"That was fast."

"A confession is in order," she said. "I was praying you'd call, felt it in my bones you would. The night we left you, we put our heads together and began thinking of ways you could join us without fallout."

"I've been wracking my brain, too."

"Early came up with an idea. Getting you in and out undetected was the major problem. You might need to write this down. Got pencil and paper?"

"Ready. Fire!"

"Drive toward Tchula. Just north of Tchula is a stretch of land called the Morgan Brake National Wildlife Reserve. It runs on the east side of Highway 49 for several miles." You got all of that?"

"So far."

She continued. "On the west side of Highway 49, not far outside of Tchula, about two or three miles, is a turnoff. It's not really a road, but it looks like a road. Hunters use it to park. Illegal, of course, but they do it."

"If it's illegal, we should pick another place."

"Have you forgotten, Hon?" she said with playful sarcasm. "This is Mississippi. They don't arrest white folks for hunting on a reserve. Just us blacks, for hunting nothing. You could stop and wait for us. We won't stop if any traffic is moving. Tchula's too dangerous. The Movement's having as many problems there as it is in Greenwood."

"Yeah, I know."

"So, it's set. Tomorrow," she said, her voice firm. "The time!" It was not a question but a foregone imperative.

"Seven o'clock," I said. "Not as much stirring then."

"Seven o'clock," she confirmed. "We'll see you then. This is good, the old gang together again. The only person missing is Uncle Giles. He'd be ecstatic."

"I still can't believe this is happening."

"Believe," she said with conviction.

When I hung up, the shakes were gone. I'd committed risking everything achieved in my life to that point. I was going where others would not go, giving what they would not give.

I felt strangely calm.

12

Tuesday, July 14.

The next morning, I drove slowly through Mt. Pleasant. Papers still lay in yards but at six o'clock much of the town was awake. Streets were wet from the sprays of the street cleaner and pickups were lining up on the main drag, tailgates down and covered with produce for sale. The men at Ivy Lee's gas station were hunched over, hunkering down on the latest. Even if the topic was old, to them it was always the latest. The windows at Ruby's Cafe were foggy with grease smoke. Old ladies wearing bonnets were bent over flowerbeds, clippers in hand and baskets at their sides. They observed my passing and my wave to them. They did not wave back. Weeks before, they had stopped, and stood, swept the air with a grand wave. On the car radio, Dylan was singing, "The times they are a changin'."

I drove west to Blackhawk, turned south on State 17 to Acona and followed the same route that had taken me to Mount Holy Rest. Past Acona, a short-cut gravel road took me to State 12 and into Tchula. Highway 49 was a major artery running the length of the state. Little traffic was about that day as I turned north in Tchula. Within a few minutes, on my right a sign slid by: MORGAN BRAKE NATIONAL WILDLIFE REFUGE. I began looking for the meeting place. It would be on the other side of the highway and in the uninterrupted wall of timber and brush, easy to spot. It was a turn-off, as Sharon had described, that thinned into what must have been a logging road at one time.

I turned, parked and waited.

Minutes later, coming from the direction of Tchula, a dark green station wagon appeared sputtering up the highway with two people in it. The car was the same one Early and Sharon drove to Mount Holy Rest. No cars were behind them. I looked north. None there either. The vehicle backfired as it slowed, turned and pulled over.

Early was driving. Sharon motioned with her arm from the passenger window. I made sure my doors were locked and then moved quickly to their car. The back door groaned loudly when I opened it.

"Have to slam it hard," Early said. "It won't catch sometimes." I thought a good dose of oil would help, but said nothing. He was looking straight ahead, and I detected an edge in his voice.

Sharon turned to face me as I slid in. "Well! That was easy enough," she said with a bright smile. She was wearing a white, long sleeved shirt rolled to her elbows and a red bandanna tied around her head, her hair falling around her shoulders.

"Next time, we'll make it a little harder and have you jump in at a slow crawl," she laughed, "Like in the good old days with Uncle Giles' wagon."

"Yeah, like in the good old days," I said. "Hope we don't get a chance to try it."

Early was still quiet, sullen. He wore overalls and a khaki shirt. His hands gripped the steering wheel as we picked up speed. The morning wind whipped coolly through the windows. Sharon made a comment about my new blue jeans, that they'd be evidence by the end of the day. At first, I didn't catch what she meant by "evidence."

"You need to bring a change of clothes next time," she continued. "We don't want you getting out at your parsonage looking like you've been building a church. Actually we're tearing it down so we can rebuild."

I nodded, distracted briefly by the man's shirt she was wearing. I guessed it was Early's.

Most of the way, Sharon talked, bringing me up to date about recent events in Greenwood and the Freedom Day arrests. The mass arrest victims from Drew were still in the Greenwood city jail and the Leflore County penal farm awaiting trial. A shotgun had been fired at a fellow worker's car. Early injected a comment from time to time, but otherwise, he remained silent. He seemed morose and dejected. Something was troubling him. Sooner or later, it would come out. I hoped sooner. I did not know this companion, blood brother from my childhood.

The Bethel brick church was a charred shell. The roof, except for a few rafters, was gone, the windows blown out. A back wall was braced by a chimney and the side walls were intact. The chimney, I reasoned, had doubled as a fireplace and a stove in earlier days of the church's life. The brick foundation across the front looked solid but was disconnected from the front steps.

Several pickups were backed up to the ruins, people throwing burned debris into the beds. No one was sitting. Everyone was working. Most were black, a few whites, but no faces I remembered from the evening at Mount Holy Rest. I thought Brodsky and Rubin might be there and was told later they were organizers, working the territory for voter registration. Their time spent on that task more valuable than helping rebuild a church. I wondered about the value placed on our work then decided who was doing what was not relative. We were all bodies on the line, each a potential target.

Early pulled off to the side of the church under a stand of pines and parked. Sharon unfolded from the car and shut the door with her hip. Her shirt and jeans seemed to melt into her. I hoped her work didn't require much bending. She went to the rear of the station wagon, opened the back and retrieved pairs of work gloves. The thought of needing gloves never occurred to me.

"Don't worry," she said, noting my look of exasperation. "I put in two extra pairs for you."

The gloves recalled my rides with Giles and helping him unload slab wood. "You learned that from Uncle Giles," I said. "He always kept an extra pair for us."

She gave a knowing smile.

"But two?" I said.

"You've never cleaned up a burned building before?" she said.

"And you have?"

"Three. Two churches and one house."

I had forgotten. Her house had burned when she was ten years old, not long after I'd met her. I remember the day Lula told me and how I had waited with a stopped heart for the words, "No one was at home." Was this the special bond with Early? I imagined their first date, what they might have talked about. Fires. Things lost. Things saved. His scars and silly grin. That's what I missed most about him, the grin. I hadn't seen one crease his face since the night at the church in the car before the conversation turned serious.

He was standing by his open door observing me observing her, then slammed it and said "Come on. We got work to do."

*　*　*

For three days, we worked steadily, cleaning away the wreckage and rubble, raking and bagging ashes, unhinging charred timbers and boards and breaking and cleaning bricks that would be reused. In the distraction of hard work, my imagined fears dissipated in the heat and sweat. I got to know faces by first names quickly and came to understand the spirit that held this family and the Movement, together. I learned freedom songs till I could sing them by heart. I thought of a people long ago singing in fields, their messages carried by the songs, as clear as drumbeats in the African jungle, and I knew where the spirituals were born, the songs my children and theirs would sing for all time.

The hours varied but usually ran from early morning until dusk. Sharon had pulled her hair back into a ponytail revealing the fuller features of her face. She always prepared enough lunch for the three of us, which recalled other days of wax paper lunches—bologna sandwiches, deviled eggs and Oreos. We drank iced tea poured from gallon jugs into paper cups and well water brought to us in a galvanized pail from a neighbor's house. The second day, small children accompanying parents found a dewberry patch and we broke long enough to enjoy the luscious tartness of the berries. Someone brought a jar of bacon grease to rub on chigger bites. I brought some mosquito repellent, but only the white workers seemed to need it. "Mosquitoes don't bite us colored folks," said one of the black women.

After several days, Early seemed to loosen up and became more congenial. Perhaps, he saw how hard I was working and realized my effort was for real and not just token. He still glowered when Sharon and I rested and visited together. She must have noticed too, or they had talked. By the second day, she was keeping more to herself. She took breaks with Early or others of their group, leaving me to fend for myself. From time to time, I'd notice her looking at me and found myself catching glimpses of her, too, the pillared legs, how her tapered figure moved through the heat shimmer when she walked, how her earrings danced when she threw back her head. Watching her face became a habit with me. I wanted to penetrate the rich darkness behind it and see for myself what was there. I hoped the chance would come when we could be together.

These thoughts weighed on me at night as I lay awake. The frightful fact I was white and she was black seemed of little concern. I didn't notice, or want to notice, the ease with which I was crossing a dangerous line. Looking back, I'd done it all before. On a block that didn't fit the norm.

I did think I'd found a friend.

I worried about my absence from the parish, but made up for lost time by visiting in the evenings and arising early each morning to clear out paperwork. I worked on sermons late at night and while driving back and forth. The challenge of the manual work away from the mental work and the risk I was taking created an energy I'd never before felt.

Early and Sharon picked me up and returned me to my car each day without a hitch. I became braver, or more foolish. On Friday at the end of the first week, I told them to let me out with traffic zipping both ways. No car slowed. No one seemed to notice or care. I told them good-bye, knowing it would be a long weekend before I would join them again. Sharon was about to say something as I closed the door but Early interrupted and made a vague comment about needing to hurry. She made the little trill with her fingers and smiled. I'd told myself if she looked back, it meant she cared.

As they drove away, she turned and glanced back.

13

Monday, July 20

This time, Sharon came to the burned church by herself. Early had to return to school in Jackson, something about his class schedule and a scholarship she told me. She didn't go into details, and I didn't press. There were no cars coming when I got in and closed the door, but I slumped down in the seat. I was riding up front with a female driver who was black. I was begging for trouble.

After the initial conversation about Early, she said nothing else, her eyes hard and vigilant on the highway. I sensed there was more to the reason Early wasn't there, but I left the issue alone. The Beatles were screaming about *A Hard Day's Night* on the radio.

"That's a Mississippi disc jockey for you," she said with an edge of contempt.

"How's that?" We were both from Mississippi, but somehow I took the comment personally.

"'Where Did Our Love Go'?' is second on the top five and the Beatles 'A Hard Day's Night' third, but they're all you hear."

"So. Who sings 'There Goes Our Love'"?

"It's 'Where Did Our Love Go?' and it's sung by the"—she looked at me and flashed an exaggerated smile— "Suu-premes."

She changed the subject and asked me about my weekend. I took her through the steps of typing and preparing a mimeograph template and

Sunday's bulletin. I gave her a rundown of my visitation schedule and the interesting personalities in my congregations. I rambled on, probably telling her more than she wanted to know. She seemed interested but kept her eyes on the road.

Most of the cleanup at the church had been completed. The rest was tedious and monotonous. We cleaned bricks with files, chisels and screwdrivers, anything hard and sharp that would respond to the tap tapping of a hammer or hatchet, which we also used to break up the conglomerates. Separate stacks had been designated. Whole bricks in one pile, half bricks in another and fragments in a third. With two wheelbarrows and a system, we watched the stacks grow. Someone said building the church could begin in a few days, that a wealthy black from Clarksdale had donated several thousand dollars to get us started, and that SNCC had negotiated with COFO for another five thousand.

"Why wait several days?" I asked Sharon at lunch break. "The rate we're cleaning these bricks, we could start tomorrow. And the weather's with us."

"It's supplies," she said. "Nobody around here will sell to us. We thought we had a deal with a lumberyard in Greenwood, then somebody threw a smoke bomb on the owner's front lawn. They're checking at several other places—Greenville, Lexington, Indianola, as far south as Jackson. Something will turn up. It always has," she said, a sparkle in her eyes.

Sharon and I ate lunch on a grassy spot beneath the pines, the only time we'd been together all day. It was hot, the sun hammering the yard. Thin branches overhead offered little relief. Tiny droplets of sweat beaded on her forehead and ran down her temples. She seemed to brood over her food, as though it were a sacrament she dare not waste. I'd felt a distance between us since we had arrived that morning. Limited contact on the work site. Fewer glances from her. Perfunctory pats on the shoulder instead of touches that carried affection. Perhaps the problem was my perspective, my heightened expectations based on Early's absence. She spent part of the morning break with another female volunteer, motioning me away as though I were intruding upon secret woman talk. I even decided I was being selfish and attributed her aloofness to her intense focus and dedication. Perhaps later, we would have more time together.

We finished the day. All stacks were completed. A volunteer held the last brick high in his hand. We cheered and applauded as he ceremoniously placed it atop a large square stack several feet high. People began picking up their tools and heading for their cars and pickups. I began to do the same, except I was riding with Sharon. We'd be the last to leave.

When I'd done all I could do, I walked to the steps that led to nowhere and sat down. My feet could use the break. I could still feel the day's heat from the hard baked ground through my soles.

I watched as Sharon, like a good crew leader, went from person to person, patting shoulders, hugging and waving good-byes. Some of the faces triggered recollections of kindness. The old woman, her name was Mary, who trudged back each day bringing fresh well water from a house down the road. She was a short, stout woman with a plain wide face. She wore the same print dress, armpits dark with sweat, and white socks collapsed around her ankles and the same tennis shoes sliced along the sides to ease her swelling feet. She was white and either didn't know what she was risking or knew and didn't care.

There was the young bearded man who found, buried in the rubble and ashes, the brass cross that had adorned the altar. He took it with him and brought it back the next day, not good as new, but cleaned and polished and ready for future services. His last name was Rubenstein. The white high school twins who came each afternoon with cookies their invalid mother had baked. The eighty-year-old Negro woman who came faithfully each day and cleaned bricks.

I watched the last cars and trucks depart. The sun, moving through shades of orange to red and crisscrossed with darting chimney swifts, was setting over the timber tops in the distance. Across the road beyond the pastures, pink mists gathered along the tree rows. To the north, an evening star shone and in the southern sky another, both bright and shimmering in the heat rising from the land. Between those brilliant points of light, the sky lay as though bruised by another hard day.

I sat and waited.

Sharon waved to the last car then with that stately, wide-strided patrician gait walked to the car. I thought of royalty, of a Nile queen returning to her royal barge after surveying a day's work on a valley pyramid or temple. I gave little thought to what she was doing until she got in the car and started it. She had not even looked at me. Had she become so intensely focused she'd forgotten about me? Was she leaving me? I watched as she backed up, drove the car behind the rear wall of the church and parked it. I heard the door slam and turned around to see what she was doing.

Shortly, she emerged through a door of the rear wall and began walking toward me. The sun was to my back. Into my long shadow, through the voided sanctuary, she moved, her beauty something unlikely in that place, I thought, or really any place. Her face was expressionless in the dusk glow, and I tried to read in her countenance any disposition of what was coming next. Had I done something wrong? Was I in for a lecture? Was Early fed up and I was going to hear about it? Was this goodbye? I sat there completely confused, no clue what was going on. Then she stopped, curled a finger and motioned for me.

I got up and followed.

The rear and side walls of the church were intact, leaving the front open and facing the road. She led me into a far corner, one encased in shadow and less visible from the road. Swiping a foot over the ground, she cleared away rubble, sat down and motioned for me to join her.

To this point, nothing had been said. Not a word uttered. The silence was eerie, unsettling.

We sat at right angles, she leaning against one wall, I another, our legs outstretched, our feet almost touching. Twilight was drawing across the landscape, the sun's last rays shining through the trees across the road casting an arabesque shade upon us. I thought of faraway summer dusks and the end of other long glorious days, sitting across from her in the bed of Giles' wagon as it slowly made its way beneath the shaded streets, heading to my house to drop me off.

Finally, she spoke. "Sam Ransom." She let out a long sigh. "We've just needed time to talk. And this is about as good as any."

We did need to talk. I needed to talk—about her, about Early, about his attitude. About why she'd ignored me all day and the previous Friday. About why she'd been so quiet, so withdrawn. About how I was feeling abandoned. But this was her idea. She'd orchestrated the day to this one fine point. It didn't take much to get her started. As I'd done many times in the days of our youth, I nodded and said, "You first."

She lunged.

She said she needed to tell me things she could tell no one. She told me of divisions within the movement, great fundamental rifts. She spoke of those who advocated violence, those who advocated non-violence and the negotiators in the middle trying to hold it together. She did not have to tell me she belonged to the latter. She told me of secret plans in the violent-prone camp to sabotage efforts by those in the non-violent camp. She said at times the tension veered dangerously close to war within the larger war. She told of in-fighting and turf battles and petty jealousies among the workers.

At one point, she reached over, grabbed my hand and held it. A warmth spread downward from my face into my chest, my loins. I'd felt the touch of other hands, of other women. Hands that were dainty and lotion soft. Hands that had been pampered, indulged and had their own way. Hands that were white.

At first, her hand's smooth palm spreading over the top of my hand seemed no different. Then I reached over and placed my hand over hers, only briefly, but long enough to sense its leathery feel, the rough knuckles, calluses along the edges. As I withdrew my hand, I knew I had felt one that had known work and drudgery, a hand that had given more than it had received. A hand that had suffered.

I took her gesture as a touch of confidence. I was someone she could trust. There were questions I wanted to ask, but her intensity barred interruption. Her hand still on mine, I continued listening, waiting, as she peeled back the frustrated layers of her outer self, hoping, at some point, she'd start touching the nerves of her inner world.

And she did.

I was relieved I didn't have to ask.

Yes, Early was jealous of her relationship with me, a jealousy, I was unaware of, that spanned the years of our childhood. As I had suspected, there were also problems between the two of them, fundamental differences, before I re-entered their lives. Early wanted to vent anger; she wanted to solve problems. He said Martin Luther King's pacifist approach was a sign of weakness, that he was playing into racist hands with his "nonviolent shit." She disagreed and said that pacifism was a quiet strength which would eventually triumph in the long march. Whenever she countered him, he lost his temper, like he did that night in the car. Their relationship was already in decline; "deteriorating" was the word she used.

She told me she was fed up. She told me she was tired and lonely. She told me when she saw me that night at Mount Holy Rest she didn't know when or how He would do it, or who He would send, but that God had answered a prayer.

"Early was not glad to see me?" I had to ask.

"He was at first," she said. "Seeing you, a familiar face, was a pleasant shock. Driving back that night he said how good it was to see you again. He talked about how it took courage for you to come to the meeting. He interpreted some of your comments as waffling, but when you called that you were joining us, he got excited. I believe he was really proud of you."

"Then …"

She squinted up into the dark tops of the trees backlit by the fading dusk sky and slow-blooming stars. "Then, I think history took over. He remembered too much of the past, the games we had played, the stories we had acted out. How you were usually the one who saved me, protected me, hovered over me. He knew I liked you then, thought you were cute."

She paused, then continued. "I was probably some to blame. I made too much out of seeing you and having you on our team. Before we even picked you up on the first day, his feelings were changing. Whenever I made a positive comment about you, he'd come back with a negative. He began to see you as a co-conspirator, one more trooper on the other side he'd have to fight to get to the real fight. Early has trouble getting over the past … all of it." She stopped and released my hand.

The sun had completely set, the night accomplished, the moon not yet risen, the tree line across the road a black palisaded wall against the lighter sky. We sat in a hot, fecund dark that seemed to lie down around us, the air rich and damp, the shrill cicadas droning off the trees. An intensity filled the air, the kind that says, regardless of efforts to prevent it, something is going to happen.

I couldn't see her face, only the outline of her head. Her body was right angled to mine, a light-colored shape there in the walled dark. The ground was still warm and heat radiated from the brick wall against my back, but cool breezes were beginning to ventilate the sanctuary's gutted shell.

Above us, on a ragged square of clear sky rimmed by the outline of the ruined walls, bright stars twinkled like sequins on a swatch torn from the original.

For a while I said nothing, her final comment about Early still resonating in my mind. I knew now why she'd kept her distance, why her collaboration with me was as problematic for her as my risky involvement in the project was for me. I was an outsider, and for all I knew considered by some in her group, a spy.

"That explains a lot," I finally said missing her hand on mine.

"Not everything," she said.

"No, it doesn't." I sensed the discussion moving toward deeper water and decided to steer it to more comfortable depths. "Do you remember—" The question began and suddenly, from nowhere, headlight beams, sweeping the walls of the church and nearby trees and boring on into the dark. We watched the taillights fade, like bright red eyes in the humid summer night.

"Is it safe for us to be here?" I said.

"Safer here than anywhere else."

"What if a car comes from the other direction?"

"The road from that direction is straight."

She'd no sooner spoken than we heard, coming from that direction the sound of an approaching vehicle, a distant sibilance growing to a roar as headlights came boiling out of the dark, the rumbling pickup churning gravel and raising clouds of dust as it entered the curve and passed, the roar fading back to whisper and into the choruses of the night.

All was quiet again.

Neither of us spoke.

With a small intake of breath, she rose. She looked first through the window space immediately above us then toward the door in the rear wall.

"The car," she said.

"It was a pickup."

"No. Our car."

"What about it?" I said. "You pulled it around back."

"Yes. I just wondered if passing lights could catch its taillights."

"You said the road was straight."

"It is, from where we are," she said.

"Well, the car's behind us, on the other side of the wall."

She continued standing, thinking. For the first time I saw what fear could do to her, and the heightened vigilance it evoked. "I guess you're right. I got all frenzied for nothing. But I'm glad I got up. Come, look."

She extended a hand and pulled me up beside her and there, through the damaged frame of what had been a window, within a purple tapestry of leaves and branches, a quarter moon, like a soft shell of light, was beginning its ascent into the velvet night.

"It's gorgeous," she said. "It looks like a solitary ornament hanging between the branches. I've always wondered why the moon is brighter at midnight when it's so much smaller and higher in the sky. I mean, that's a quarter moon and in a few hours you could read a book out here."

"It's the refraction of light waves passing through the atmosphere," I offered. "That's how the color changes, or so I've been told."

She looked at me, her light caramel face bronzed in a shaft of silver. "Whatever it is, it's simply gorgeous." She smiled briefly, her lips full.

I wasn't focused on the moon but what its luminance did to her, the way it defined and sharpened her long columned legs, the curvature of her hips, her breasts; the way it struck the classic angles of her face. I didn't think I'd ever seen anything more beautiful. Standing there looking at her, at those images, it hit me. The name. Her name. The thought had been flickering around the rim of my consciousness, like something one might see from the tail of an eye. Her last name was Word, but she was named for someone in the Bible. The connection sent a shudder through me. I wanted to tell her I knew, but not then. Later. When the time was right.

We sat down, back into the shadows. This time she sat next to me, our bodies almost touching.

"Where were we?" she said, her voice as soft as her smile.

"I had begun a question, 'Do you remember—' Then the car came. I was going to ask if you remembered the first time you saw me."

"My, that was a long time ago," she said.

"It was nineteen fifty-two."

"You're probably right," she said. "I didn't think in terms of years back then. I barely do now, though this one I won't forget. I can remember *where* better than *when*. I can't see when, but I can see where. Where is like a time frame I can stop, freeze in my mind's eye and in it see objects, people, images that are like anchors for me. To answer your question, Uncle Giles and I are in his wagon coming down the street—"

"—I'm sitting on the curb."

She nodded and continued, her head tilted back, her eyes closed, "and I see Early sitting with you in front of your house. It is a two-story brick and frame structure with a wrap-around front porch. Cement steps lead up into the yard and you are looking up at us—you are, not Early—like you don't believe what you see, like what you see had just dropped down from heaven."

"Heaven is right," I said. "Riding with Giles was as close to heaven on earth as we could get." I could never calculate age well but thought him to be somewhere in his fifties. "Is he still hauling slab wood?"

"He was the last time I was home," she said. "He's probably stopping at the same places, probably has other young passengers."

"I remember the last time I saw you, the place better than the time."

"I don't remember either, where or when," she said solemnly. "Maybe I've repressed it."

"You were standing in the back of the wagon going down Cleveland Street. Early and I were standing on the sidewalk in front of my house, the same place where I first saw you. It was the week before my twelfth birthday. I felt something leaving me I could not bring back. I never saw you again until that night at the church. I've thought of you often and would say to myself, 'Whatever happened to Sharon Rose? Where did she go?' I wondered which side you'd eventually come down on. Sorry, Sharon, but you—"

"Call me Shar. That's what I go by now. I like the shorter sound. Like Sam. It's more me."

I couldn't repeat the name right away, its awkward newness. I would wait later when it was genuine and not an echo. "To me, you never looked like one of them. Your color seemed closer to mine." Immediately, I regretted the remark and knew I was opening up that *long story for another time* she'd been dodging. But that other time, so elusive before, seemed unavoidably upon us, inexorably, as though all that had gone before was pushing us to this ripe point and the words just popped out. I didn't know how she would react.

"'Like one of them,'" she said tartly. It was a verbal slap, but spoken in a whisper. "That's the way white people think. Everyone should look like them."

She was still whispering, as though she might be overheard. Her breath was loud after she spoke. She gave me a hard look, one that cut through the dark, one that meant every word she said. Her eyes were nailing mine, then looked away.

"That's not what I meant," I said.

"I know. But you were raised in that culture, just as I was in mine. I could be white as a Sunday tablecloth, but I was raised black. You could be dark as the other side of the moon, but if you were raised white, you'd feel white. You'd think white." Her natural voice returned but the edge was still there.

I turned and looked back at her. Her face was in mine as though she had more to say. She was still breathing hard but she stopped, turned and faced the night. "I guess I would at that. I'm sure I feel and think white. But, Shar, that doesn't keep my thoughts and feelings from crossing over." Calling her Shar didn't feel right, but I guessed I'd get used to it, like she did Sam. To me, she would always be Sharon Rose.

"I know," she said. "That's how I came into this world. My daddy was white. *Was.* He's dead now. My mama worked for him. He was a doctor." She turned toward me, her face half in shadow, half in moonlight. "I won't tell you his name, but you know him," and she turned away again. "He screwed her when she'd come to the house to work and then he got unlucky. She became pregnant. She refused to let him perform an abortion. He was going to turn his back on her and she threatened to tell his wife. Of course, she quit working for him, but he continued paying her, slipping her cash. She'd have to go to his office to get it. Then he died and that's when we went to Indiana. My mother had a sister there who found a good job for her. You know the rest of the story. I came back."

I didn't know the rest of the story, but I made some deductions. I remembered her mother was light-colored, too, and that Sharon was probably the product of a practice long in play before she was born. I spent no time trying to guess the name of the doctor. I did not want to know. But I did want to know about something else. The time was right.

I turned, looked at her and said, with no inflection of question, "Lily of the valleys."

Her eyes snapped on me as though I'd pried open something private. I couldn't decipher the look, if she was angry or hurt, neither, or some other emotion sprung suddenly to life within her in that moment.

"The rose of Sharon," she said, her eyes still flared with surprise, but her voice was even.

"Your mother named you for her."

She hesitated, as though thinking through her response. "Yes. King Solomon's dark lover in his Song of Songs." She lifted her eyes toward the sky as though nothing more needed to be said.

And for a while, nothing was said as though something of time and history hung in the air, something that spoke of the creation and its ethnic groans, the taboo of the species. We sat there ensconced in the corner staring at the sky, at the brilliance of the rising moon pouring down, at the bright stars in the periphery of its light, looking at anything but at each other as though we were afraid to look.

Then, she laid a hand gently on my thigh, turned again and looked at me. The night had straightened the trees. The moon was higher, its light beating down on the leaves. I could see her face, her dark eyes searching my face, eyes that, as I looked into them, had no bottom. No breeze rang special chimes in the trees. The moon did not come from behind a cloud. No nightingale sang a special note.

I had assumed that love would come to me some day. It would happen in a church or at a reception, eyes meeting across a crowded room. There would be this instantaneous, unmistakable acknowledgement, cast and recast nonverbally and I would, with the same spontaneity, act upon it. I did not know it would happen in a place that was burned out, in a gutted sanctuary. I did not know my nerves would be stripped and my mind freeze, but I would not question, even slightly doubt, its validity. I tried to carry on as though there'd been no tremendous upheaval inside of me and glad she picked up the thread, even though it had a negative twist.

"You know it would never work," a deep vertical groove between her eyebrows giving her an intense look.

I knew then I should not worry about Sharon Rose, Shar, making it in life. Not the way she could cut through the anatomy of something and plunge straight to the raw nerves.

"So, you feel the same about me," I said.

"I don't know. I'm not sure what I feel. I know when I saw you that night at Mount Holy Rest something clicked. Maybe it was seeing the comforting face of an old friend, a connection of memories, those days, that place." She stretched out her feet and touched mine. "You remember," she said. It was not a question.

"I remember. Uncle Giles got all over you for messin' with me."

"And I told him you were messin' with *me*," she countered.

We relived those days in the wagon again and laughed, shared our feelings, ran our minds over them, probing and testing like mountain climbers for secure points to take us higher, safely. Above us, cicadas buzzed as though an alarm had gone off setting in motion things that could not be stopped.

She shifted to the side and propped her legs casually across mine. "At least, it wouldn't work around here," she said.

"I'm not so sure of that. I hear the volunteers mix. Whites and blacks are dating. Some are sleeping together. Right here in Mississippi."

"I know," she replied. "But this is different. You are a white minister with a white congregation. I don't think they'd take too kindly to a preacher's colored wife."

A sudden quiet filled our space. We were not looking at each other. We'd been speaking to the moon's horn riding the night and the sky throbbing with stars. I caught a whisper of her perfume. My entire body was burning with awareness of her. I wanted to kiss her. My desire for her was like a bomb exploding under water. Not now, I said to myself.

I waited.

She waited.

In the delicate silence, we both waited. In an air full of certainty that sooner or later passion was going to erupt, one of us would make the first move. Looking back on those moments, I think of great love scenes in the movies, the tension before the first touch, the first kiss, two people assessing their courage, the risk. Then she leaned against me and reached for my hand. I opened it to her, felt her long fingers intertwine mine, relished the way they slid and locked into place and enjoyed the thrill traveling my spine, touching my loins. I wanted those long slender, red-tipped spears to rip and tear me apart.

I did not have to wait long.

In the ravenous silence, her lips and mouth were suddenly on mine, her tongue pushing through my teeth, probing my mouth, starved. All I remember are the rivers of sweat pouring from my body, a blade of moonlight across hers, her feathering of my pubescent pulse, the explosion, the lingering odor of something burned, a choir of whippoorwills when we were through and the cicadas taking up again ringing in my ears like a fever.

14

Tuesday, July 21

The rest of the week, Early was back. I felt confident Sharon had said nothing to him. The three of us worked side by side as though nothing had happened. I rationalized I'd violated no code of honor or of friendship. Though they'd been close at one time, the relationship between Early and Sharon had changed. His feelings for her were different than hers for him. This, she had assured me. I should not be concerned that ours developed so quickly. We were in a situation where everything, of necessity, moved faster, relationships made and broken overnight within that hot sweltering pressure.

The latter, at times, weighed on my insecurities. I could lose her in a star blink. Then I'd recall the years of our youth and thought not. Whenever any of us encounter relationships of old, class reunions come to mind, we tend to measure ourselves by where we were at that time, as though a part of us is locked into that frame and we cannot step out of it. Wherever Early, or anyone else, came into the equation, I'd always be her first love. That was what I told myself, reassured myself.

The feelings I had for Early were on a different level. A course in Greek had helped me learn I could compartmentalize love. There was *agape* or spiritual love, which functioned within me when I was preaching and helping others. *Eros* needs no further comment. Then there was *philos*, loving/liking another, a bondage of friendship. My love for Early I'd obviously consigned to this latter definition. But for Sharon and me? Our relationship defied any category. I thought our love was a special *agape,* but it was all over the place.

Much further along in life, I understand now that love with another embodies all three of the Greek meanings. At that time, I was living out of one emotional compartment at a time, a one-man damage control on guilt, moving my reasoning here and there and trying to stay one step ahead of condemnation, of judgment. I deluded myself by thinking I was getting closer and closer to redemption. I even began to wonder which came first. Is it guilt then forgiveness or forgiveness then guilt? The two were hand-in-hand, a symbiosis, like the proverbial snake that feeds on itself.

One particular guilt—sex before marriage—gnawed inward from the origins of my culture and faith. I was not a virgin, so this guilt was not new. And guilt, like anger, if we don't trash it early on, accumulates. Some tapes in our mind are not easily erased.

*   *   *

My first sexual experience occurred when I was a junior in high school. The year was 1957. I'd heard rumors about Ramona Littlejohn. She was a dark-haired, long-thighed, high-bosomed, six-foot sophomore Amazon beauty who could strip a basketball net from center court. She lived in a house trailer on a back lot off Highland, one street over from me. She had these powerful model's legs that flirted with each other when she walked. So, when I stood behind her at the drink fountain one day and she raised up, literally head and shoulders above me, I looked up and asked if she'd go with me to the drive-in movie. The drive-in was brand spanking new, something I thought, her opinion of my dwarfish status aside, she could not resist.

And she did not.

Two things I recall about the movie: its name, *Peyton Place,* and one of the actresses. Not her matinee name, but her movie name, Nellie Cross, her tan beauty and the problems she created by dating a boy who was white. Years later, when I tried my hand at writing and choosing names for characters, I thought of Nellie Cross.

Minister to be or not, I knew, deep down in my blood and bones, what I'd done that night was wrong, yet, somehow, in that knowing it was wrong, I knew I was going to do it again.

I asked and Sharon agreed to meet again, Saturday night, same place. We took the same precautions. We made love again, in the same spot, this time under a full moon. The word love was never spoken. Very little, in fact, was said. It was not that words were not needed; we knew none.

15

Sunday, July 26

Logic and reason abandoned, I drove straight from my last Sunday service to Bethel Church. Due to evening services at Mount Holy Rest and Redbone, both nearby, there was more traffic than usual, so I made several passes before turning into the church yard. I arrived first and parked behind the rear wall. The radial hands on my watch said nine o'clock. I waited.

Thirty minutes went by.

An hour.

No sign of Sharon.

Thinking I had been detained, had she come and gone? Surely not. She knew my last service was not far away. Maybe she got held up or couldn't get the car, or Early insisted on coming and she aborted. These scenarios and others raced through my mind. Approaching headlights signaled her arrival only to pass, leaving empty whirls of dust. Every vehicle that came along the road that night went past ... went past ... went past ....

Eleven o'clock.

Still no sound or sign of her. Of anyone.

A ruined dark surrounded me, the sky overhead pricked with stars, heavy like a perforated lid. Moonlight became a menace, a threat. The sounds of the woods began to saw on my nerves. I would wait until eleven thirty, I told myself.

Somewhere, a dog was barking.

Then quiet.

Eleven thirty.

I started the car and began backing up to turn around. I was fully turned and saw headlights. Not coming from the south, as expected, but from the north, from Blackhawk. Quickly, I backed behind the rear wall. The lights slowed and bounced into the yard. The car was unfamiliar, not the one Sharon and Early had been driving.

I panicked.

I pressed the accelerator and raced toward the road. I glanced at the car passing me, caught a blur of the driver's face and slammed on the brakes. It was Sharon. I turned, followed her and pulled up beside her behind the wall. She jumped from her car, rushed toward me and grabbed me as I was getting out. The impact almost knocked me down. She clung to me and began sobbing.

"What's wrong? For God's sake, what's wrong?"

"It's horrible," she cried punching away a tear with her knuckles. "Just hold me. Just hold me."

I held her trembling shoulders, breathed into her perfumed hair. I waited and tried again. "When you feel like talking, I'm ready to listen."

Sniffling through a runny nose, she whimpered, "I know, thank you."

I pulled out a handkerchief she quickly accepted.

"Bad news from home?" I attempted.

She took a step back and blew her nose. "No. Just give me a minute."

She blew again. "Our car was bombed outside the home where we're staying."

"My God."

"That's not the worst of it. Early's in the hospital in Greenwood. That's where I've been."

"What happened?"

"He's not hurt," she said. "Nothing like that. Not yet, anyway. Do you know the name Silas McGhee?"

"Yeah, the young Negro whose been trying to integrate the theater in Greenwood."

"Well, he and his brother, Jake, were mobbed by a hundred or more whites as they left the theater today. They were cut up pretty bad and got glass in their eyes when somebody," she paused and wiped her eyes, "threw a Coke bottle through the window of the car taking them to the hospital, which is where Early comes in. He was at the theater trying to help. I warned him, told him we should just stick to voter registration and rebuilding the church, but that only made him mad and he said he had to do his thing." She took a deep breath and tried to calm her shakes. "The SNCC bunch has influenced him. He likes their brand of confrontation. Now all of them are trapped in the Leflore County Hospital. Cars of armed whites have blocked the roads leading into and out of the hospital. The FBI and police won't do anything. They're even refusing protection."

"Just Early and the McGhee brothers?" I pressed.

"No. He's there with other SNCC staff."

"That's why you came from the direction of Blackhawk. Were you hurt?"

"No. Well, just emotionally," she said still shaking. "The hospital faces the river and there are only two ways to get to it. I parked down a side street a block away and walked."

"How did you know Early was there?"

"He called from a hospital phone."

"And the car, when did all of that happen?" I probed further.

"This is the unreal part. Right before I was to leave for church, I guess about six thirty, there was still some daylight, somebody came by and threw a homemade bomb at the car. One of the Lusks, the people we stay with, had forgotten to raise the windows and lock the car as we've been warned to do, and the bomb was thrown through a window. We heard the explosion and ran out. The car was in flames and there was nothing we could do but watch it burn. Firemen finally came and put it out."

"You're lucky it didn't explode," I said.

"That's what one of the firemen said. It had just been filled up, so there was little room for gas fumes to expand in the tank to cause an explosion."

"Where did you get the car you're in now?"

"Neighbors. They let me borrow it. That's why I can't stay long. I need to get back to the hospital in case they let them go. Early will need a ride."

She drew close again and put her head against my shoulder.

"Let me go with you," I offered.

She pushed back. "Are you crazy? The last thing you or I need is to be seen together."

The words cut, but I knew she was right. I held her for a while and we kissed.

"When will I see you again?" I said in a voice almost pleading.

"Tomorrow, if you can."

"Back here? Same plan?"

"Yes and no. They're delivering supplies tomorrow from a lumber company in Yazoo City. Somebody struck a deal. The SNCC staff is bringing in some volunteer carpenters from a church in the Delta that's almost finished."

"So, it's yes?" I said.

"Yes, if they get the supplies here in daylight and don't try to unload at night."

"I'll be here."

She kissed me again and looked back as she was getting into the car. "I've told Early nothing."

"I understand."

"But he knows something's not right. It's going to be tough, Sam Ransom, being around you all day and not being able to—"

"I know. Would you rather I not come?"

"No."

"I'll be here then. We'll make the best of it."

"We're minus one car now," she lamented. "We may have to carpool with others. We won't be able to pick you up at the usual spot. What will you do about getting here?"

"I don't know. I'll cross that bridge tomorrow morning."

"If we're able to borrow another car, I'll call you," she said.

"Call me anyway. I want to know about Early."

She gave me a thumbs-up and ducked into the car. She rolled down the window and called to me. I walked over and she motioned with a crooked finger and I bent down for a final kiss.

"Take care, Sam Ransom," she said and patted my hand.

"You, too, Sharon Rose."

We shared a sadness, one greater than parting or plans gone awry. Reality had slammed into us, sooner than either of us had expected. I was not one of them, and she was not one of mine. That was the doom descending fast upon us, upon me.

I watched as her taillights dwindled to pinpoints, then faded into the darkness. Depression fell on me like a weight dropped from the sky. To fight it, I tried wringing thoughts from the future. There would be time before school started. Maybe she could come to Atlanta. Then, there was Thanksgiving, Christmas, spring holidays. I began charting our lives on a calendar as abstract as time. I entered the vacant sanctuary and stood again in our corner, upon invisible vectors where all of my life seemed drawn. Then, I got into the car and headed back to the parsonage.

She called later that night, about two a.m. The sheriff had finally agreed to follow the SNCC staff and the McGhees safely out and to their destinations. Early was safe. If she could get another car, she would meet me above Tchula at the Brake. Otherwise, I was on my own. I figured it would be the latter and went to sleep devising ways to be there in the morning, unaware, as I slept, of plans being concocted by others.

16

Monday July 27

I am still unsure how I got through the following days. I pushed myself to do the next thing—get out of bed, brush my teeth, eat breakfast, drive to the church, study scripture, work on sermon. In all honesty, I did not feel a real passion for *the cause.* I felt an obligation to help, but this was their cause, not mine. My cause had become Sharon Rose, the only real love, I thought, of my life. I questioned my commitment to the ministry, if that was even still a cause. I could not continue serving pastorates and have her—not in the South. I lay awake at night thinking I loved her and wondered which was truer, that I loved her or that I thought I loved her. Did I love her because I needed her or need her because I loved her.

I kept doing the next thing and waited.

She never called.

I decided to take my chances and go to the church alone.

I waited until after eight in the morning to leave the parsonage. People were moving about the town that time of day and I needed to be seen. I stopped by the church first, as I always did. Pastor beginning his daily routine. Pastor checking his mail. Pastor stopping for prayer and meditation in the sanctuary. The men from the gas station and customers entering Ruby's Cafe would see me. Anyone driving down the main thoroughfare on their way to work could see. They wouldn't know where

I went from there. Being responsible for eleven churches, some of them in the Delta, was my best cover.

I pulled into Jessup's gas station across the street. Ivy Lee came out, the perennial brown rag hanging from his side pocket and his billed cap cocked back. He asked if I wanted it filled up. I said yes, and he smiled and started the pump and began cleaning my windshield. The men sitting around were quiet but cordial. I shook their hands and tried to read their faces.

Ivy Lee finished filling up the car. "It bad needs a wash and the treads on the front right tire are done near gone," he said.

I thanked him, paid him and said I'd bring it back in a day or two. He smiled and said, "Much obliged, preacher," and I drove away.

The air was heavy and already warming. I drove through trees that shaped a column of blue sky with scattered patches of clouds. By noon, they'd be towering pillars. I glanced occasionally in the rearview but saw only the spray of dust I was leaving. Dew still glistened on leaves that bobbed along the roadside. Birds swooped in and out of the fleeting shadows. I turned on the radio. The Beach Boys sang, "I Get Around," and Johnny Rivers, "Memphis," and Barbara Streisand, "People." With Streisand, I turned it off. I wasn't feeling lucky enough to be needed, as the lyrics said, and decided I could better distract myself by singing old camp songs. I ended up humming the one song that always brought comfort. Perhaps because of the lyrics, "Comin' for to carry me home." Home was where it all began.

As I approached the church, I could see two flatbed trucks loaded with lumber and supplies. They were backed onto the grounds. I'd planned to park behind the rear wall, but the trucks blocked the passage. Around them was movement of people unloading and stacking lumber by hand. With no cranes or lifts, this chore would be an all day ordeal. I pulled beside one truck, maneuvered and backed into a shady spot near the pines, as far from the road as I could. My car would still be visible, but that was the best I could do.

A few of the volunteers gave welcome waves. One called my name. No sight of Sharon or Early. I asked someone about them, a white girl named Jessica, one who loaned us her thermos one day. She said she didn't know and told me about the firebombed car and the ordeal in Greenwood the night before. I acted surprised. She went on to say they were probably having trouble getting a ride.

I got my work gloves from the floorboard where I'd thrown a pair before leaving and began helping. It seemed half a lumberyard had been transported and deposited on the spot. Two-by-fours, two-by-sixes and four-by-fours. Boxes of nails. Rolls of black tar paper. Stacks of roofing shingles. Windows and doors. Concrete blocks. Bags upon bags of cement. Sand? No sand. You can't make cement without sand. I asked someone about the sand, and he said it was coming in the next shipment.

When would that be?

The next day or so, he replied.

Two white males were directing the unloading. I'd never seen them before and guessed they were the carpenters from the Delta. I learned later they were students from upstate New York who'd committed their summer to the Mississippi "theater," their word, as though they were the logistics support for a military campaign. The entire effort took on that aura. This was war and we were the military engineers.

Freedom songs erupted intermittently. One would die out, and another would start up. There'd be silence for a while, and then, like roundelays, the melodies began anew. I felt time had telescoped and saw us working in Delta cotton fields a hundred years before, and then again with brick and mortar in another age much further removed. I wondered if the slave songs of Egypt had really changed that much in 3,500 years. I joined in from time to time, as though I had become one of them. But I was living in a world that was not truly mine. Without Sharon and Early, I felt more a stranger than ever.

Sun and clouds rose higher and sweat ran off of me in streams. My muscles began to ache. This work was far different from raking ashen debris and cleaning bricks. I was afraid to look at my watch, afraid what the time might trigger in my mind. From the sun's angle, midday was approaching and bringing with it the unavoidable heat. I had forgotten to pack a lunch. Others would probably share theirs, but I was too embarrassed to ask. Cars and trucks passed slowly in their usual random patterns, faces gawking. Wives on errands to the nearby country store. Husbands going to and from the fields. The mailman. A tractor sputtered by, the man atop it bouncing higher in his seat. Most were white. I thanked

God for gravel roads. I could hear traffic coming and manage to duck behind a stack of bricks or lumber as it passed.

Just before we broke for lunch, an ancient grill-less Chevrolet sedan, probably once blue but faded gray, rattled into the yard and parked beside my car. It had cardboard in the back windows, a quarter-panel missing and duct tape holding a backdoor shut. A cheer went up from some of the volunteers as Early and Sharon emerged from the car. I waited on the fringe of the small cadre of excitement as the two received hugs and handclasps. Early threw his fist in the air, a gesture that had become the sign of "black power." Another cheer went up. Sharon saw me and began walking toward me. Early saw her and shot his fist once more into the air. He wasn't looking at those around him or at the ruined church and the stacked blessings surrounding it. No, he was looking straight at me. The pain of wounded friendship leveled out across that sun-bright churchyard and I knew he knew, even before she reached me, hugged me and whispered into my ear, "He knows."

I just looked at her.

"I told him," she continued, "but everything's going to be all right."

Early raised his fist again, his eyes still on me. I wondered what she meant by "all right."

The rest of the day was awkward. Sharon had packed a lunch for me and we ate together away from the pines beneath a shade of oaks on the back perimeter of the property. Early hovered nearby, but did not join us.

Sharon and I talked mostly about my car. She agreed it needed to be moved. It was impractical to drive all the way to Tchula, so she followed me to a small store three miles down the road from the church. She said it was owned by friends and that they wouldn't mind my leaving it there parked along the side of the building. If anyone asked, I could just say it quit on me. I remembered what Ivy Lee had said about the tires.

She was right about the owner's willingness to help. "Just park it back yonder," he said. "Won't nobody bother it there."

On the way back, I asked and she told me what had happened. Early had been hammering her about her disappearances and she felt she had to tell him. "It was just too much for me holding it in. Sooner or later, he was going to know. Better to get it out now."

Back at the church, I made several attempts during the long afternoon to reach out to Early. Each time, he found convenient ways to avoid me. Once, I mentioned the episode in Greenwood and told him how proud I was of him. He walked away. Sharon told me to let him stew; he'd get over it. She had a plan, she said. I didn't argue with her. I recalled a time in our childhood when Early walked away because I wouldn't play his game. He eventually came back. His persistence was memorable. Now, it was driven by passion.

Sometime mid-afternoon, I heard someone cry out. It was Early. A bee had stung him. Sharon ran immediately to him. All the years I'd known him, I'd only heard Early cry aloud once. A bee had stung him then, too.

* * *

We'd just crawled through a culvert on our hands and knees and were coming out when Early hollered. A bee had stung him on his ankle. It was on a Sunday afternoon. My mother was home, but my father had gone to the store to fix watches. He said he knew what the Bible said about working on Sundays, but it was the only time he could get his work done without having to wait on customers.

We followed my mother into the den. Besides Lula, I couldn't think of any other colored person who had been inside our house. As much as we played together, Early had never been inside mine, and I'd never been inside his. No one said our homes were off limits, but there was this feeling, one I have never been able to explain, that they were.

Early and I sat on the floor and my mother told Early to take off his shoe while she went to get her cigarettes. She said tobacco would draw out the sting. Early took off his right shoe. He wasn't wearing socks. In fact, I don't ever recall him wearing socks. He might have worn them in winter, but I only saw him in the warmer months.

We watched as my mother tore open a cigarette and pulled out the rolled joint of tobacco that broke apart in her fingers. His eyes getting bigger, Early asked if it would hurt. She told him it would take away the hurt, but his eyes grew even wider. She rolled the threads of tobacco into a ball, then mashed it between her fingers until it was flat. Next, she spit on the flattened mass and then placed it where the swelling was already beginning around the sting mark. Early flinched like my mother's treatment hurt, but he said it didn't.

Outside, clouds were gathering. The sky was growing dark and the den was growing darker.

My mother held the tobacco on Early's ankle for a few minutes and then placed a Band-Aid on it. "There, there" she said. "That should keep it in place till you get home." She gave his leg a motherly pat. There was a bright flash of lightening and a loud crash of thunder. Rain began to fall in a heavy downpour.

"He can't go home now, Mama," I said.

She nodded. "He can stay here until it quits."

Until it quits. She said it as though she were giving permission, as though permission was needed for him to stay, whether the rain quit or not, as though my mother had an urgency to get him out of the house.

"I'll call his mother and tell her he's here," my mother said.

Early shook his head.

"They don't have a telephone," I said.

My mother threw up her hands, turned and left the room. I sat there on the floor with Early. We sat Indian-style and I could see the bandage on his ankle. His head was down, and then I saw, for the second time since I'd known him, tears falling from his cheeks. I reached over and put my hand on his knee, but I said nothing this time. He wanted to be where I would have wanted to be, in his own home with his own mother.

The rain didn't let up.

The screen door banged to. My father was home.

From the den, Early and I could hear my mother telling him what had happened.

"Hell!" That was all my father said. Early and I could have said that for him. My father stepped into the den. He was still wearing his raincoat and hat. His voice was not angry. "I'll take you home now, Early." At least, he said his name, I thought at the time.

Early had quit crying. He didn't say goodbye or see you or seem to acknowledge I was even there, as though I might be the reason he got stung and was stuck at my house in a thunderstorm. He just got up and followed my father out of the room.

My father took him home. That night I heard another long fight downstairs. This time, they'd changed sides. My father didn't want Early leaving in the storm and my mother wanted him out of the house, storm or no storm.

*　*　*

One of the site workers knew the tobacco trick. I was hoping it helped better than my mother's treatment did that Sunday long ago.

By late afternoon, strong gusts of wind were bending the tops of the trees and anything not weighted down was being carried away. Nearby, dark clouds of lightning loomed. What was it I learned in high school natural science? Lightning results from a powerful clash between warm and cold air masses. "One Mississippi, two Mississippi, three Mississippi …" Giles had taught me how to measure distance from the flashes. If I couldn't get to five Mississippi before I heard thunder, the lightning flashes were less than a mile away.

"Four Mississippi" was as far as I got. One of the carpenters told everyone to stay away from anything metal and find cover. Cars were best, he said, because they sat on rubber.

Sharon and I ran to the Chevy and jumped in the front seat. She kept twisting and turning looking for Early, but he never came. He was somewhere still tending his bee sting.

Lightning was popping around us. Large drops of rain began falling and making slapping sounds on the roof of the car. The downpour was heavy and prolonged, so heavy at times we couldn't see the hood. Enclosed in a cocoon of pounding and rushing water, I became aware of a beginning erection and wanted to reach out and touch Sharon. She was behind the steering wheel, so I moved my foot over as a signal. She didn't respond.

Though she never said, she seemed absorbed in Early's emotional pain and her contribution to it.

Very little was said in that quarter hour interlude. The cardboard windows on the rear doors kept drawing our attention. They were taking a heavy beating and looked as though they would melt if they weren't blown into the car first. I asked her about the car, where they had gotten it. She said they were blessed with a supportive neighborhood. A mechanic who lived there had a few old cars and let them borrow one. He told them it burned oil and they'd have to feed it a quart every thirty miles or so, but it would get them here and back.

Cool breezes trailed the thunderstorm. The air grew hotter and steam rose from the ground. We worked another hour until the sun began setting, and then I saw a scene repeating itself, people packing up and leaving. A lonely feeling moved in with the dark. I didn't know what to do or say. I decided to just sit on the steps again and say nothing.

Sharon came over and sat down with me. Early was leaning against the car. She motioned for him to join us. With an attitude of what seemed exaggerated reluctance, he began walking toward us. Suddenly, headlights approached from the south. They entered the turn in the road, swept over Early, then Sharon and me, and passed on.

"That was close," I said.

"Too close," Early said. "I know what 'too close' is."

No one argued the point. Sharon got into the car and moved it behind the rear wall. We found a comfortable spot nearby and sat down on the ground facing the woods. I don't remember what Sharon said to kick off the discussion, but Early quickly took it away from her. When he'd finished with shots and digs at us, he launched into a tirade on the use of white volunteer workers.

"They weren't used 'til last year. Most of 'em are uppity, northeast intellectual bluebloods." His face was a knot of anger. "They're running the show and getting all the publicity, leaving us on the bottom again, like field niggers listening to whitey tell us what to do one more damn time. This is a black cause. It oughtta be run by black people," he continued fiercely.

He was on a roll and we didn't stop him. His words had weight, and he was throwing them like bombs. He railed against the NAACP and COFO for their politicking and being more interested in the Mississippi Freedom Democratic Party than the Movement, for not being more aggressive in breaking down the barriers, for conspiring against SNCC. At one point Sharon attempted humor, calling it the Student Violent Non-Coordinating Committee, but that only fueled another wave of gyrations and profanity against "white man's niggers." He saved his frontal assaults for the police, highway patrol and the Klan and Citizens Council. He paced back and forth the length of the wall, shouting and kicking trees and cursing God for making people so mean. Listening to him rant and rave, I recalled my first images of him climbing a tree and jumping onto honeysuckle vines over and over. Then later, his comment that someday he wouldn't be a "nigger" and I gained, in that remembrance, some understanding of his persistence, of the tunnel vision of his obsession.

The silences between his rantings were unnerving, the cicadas and crickets and wood frogs long muted. Knowing how sound travels at night, I moved at one point to get up and restrain him, but Sharon put out a hand and cautioned me to stay. The message on her face was clear. Let him vent. Better here than somewhere else. I understood, but wondered which anger was which and if he could tell the difference. I didn't want more left over for me when he finished.

Eventually, he wore himself down and took his place on the ground before us. "I done had my say. Y'all can talk about whatever shit you want to." In other words, *I give,* I thought.

For a while, no one spoke. I was too engrossed with all he'd said and the way he'd said it. I admired his energy and his passion. I thought about a little colored boy who wouldn't be an "injun" anymore, who, someday, was going to be somebody. I thought about the Black Knight. I still believed he would be great someday, a leader of his people. Though I thought his logic faulty in places, too laden with emotion, I felt the rough edges would smoothen and he'd make a mark on history with a softer, more compassionate touch. In that moment, I believed in him. I knew I would read about him, not as one reads about an idol, but as a hero. Idols risk little. Early had everything at stake.

Sharon diverted us to our stories, the old stories and some new old stories we'd forgotten. Sometimes there were no stories. We sat quietly, absorbed in the sights and sounds of nature and each other's company. Once again, as though transported in time, I felt us back in the old wagon, our own small world protected by its rough cypress siding and the man driving it. He was all that was missing. I thought about Giles, how proud he'd be of his three little pilgrims. We'd have to have a reunion, all of us. Get the old wagon out and hook up Bud, if he was still around. We wouldn't have to go anywhere. Just sit there in Giles' yard beneath that single tree.

And be just us.

17

No one noted the time. Above the serrated tree line, the moon was high, small and bright. Our bodies were sprawled like lotus-eaters in a tropical afternoon. I thought of Peter at the Transfiguration and wished we could freeze frame our moment together.

Suddenly, as though from nowhere, a rumble of traffic coming fast along the road, louder than a single vehicle. Immediately, we sat up. Lights slapped and bounced across the trees and a roar of motors invaded the side yard of the church. The headlights on the woods went out, but the motors were still running.

Early's reaction was instinctive. "Run, both of you, into the woods."

"You, too," said Sharon.

"No. I know what I'm doing. Go! Now! While their motors are still running. The sound'll cover you."

I wasn't going to argue. I grabbed Sharon's hand and pulled her with me. We headed toward the trees and plunged into wet brush and saplings. Branches hit me in the face and several times I almost fell backward on top of her. Our hands uncoupled, but I could hear her breathing.

"Go on. Go on," she panted. "I'm behind you."

A downward slope hurled me through thick briars and vines that tore cloth and flesh. I was breathing darkness instead of air, dodging trees by sense of feel, slapping at branches, constantly unhooking my arms and feet from sudden snares and tentacles until it all seemed so loud I had to stop.

My heart hammered in my ears. My clothes were soaked from sweat and droplets of rain still hanging on branches from the storm. I smelled the sour odor of rank earth smothered by dead leaves and decaying wood. I knelt in the soft mulch and tried to get my breath and bearings. I couldn't see and didn't know if Sharon was still behind me. Then leaves rustling to my left, soft padding of feet.

"Sam? Sam?"

"Where are you?" I whispered back.

"Over here. Stay where you are."

She moved quietly to my side. "Let's stop and see if we can hear," she said softly. "I'm afraid for Early, damn him."

"Maybe it's somebody just checking on the church."

"Listen!" she breathed.

We were about a hundred feet from the church. Flashlight beams jerked about in the dark, but that was all we could see. Male voices were barely audible. If I held my breath and exhaled slowly, I could hear their voices, their fragmented talk.

"Where the hell? ... goddamn lights ... over here."

Then someone louder. "What you doin' out here nigger?"

"Just resting," Early said. "I worked here today, too tired to drive home."

"You one of them smart ass niggers, huh?" Another voice. "Ain't got no better place to rest than behind this church?"

"Name of the church is Mount Holy Rest, Bud," another voice said.

Laughter.

"Naw, it ain't. That one's down the road," said yet another.

Laughter again.

"Look at his face, boys," said the first voice. "He done been burned onc't. This ain't one y'all torched and let get away is it?"

More laughter, taunting, derisive.

I felt sick. Nausea rose in me like sediment in a disturbed container, the congealed hatred of the land.

"We can git rid of those scars for you, boy. Cain't we, men?"

"Sure as a bear shits in the woods."

"Won't never look the same."

"Won't even know you got 'em, 'cause it'll all look the same," yet another, different snickering voice.

I was fighting back tears. Sharon was trembling on my arm and holding her hand over her mouth.

"This is sick," she whispered.

"There's no word for it," I whispered back.

"Now, I'll give you one more chance to answer my question, boy. You ain't got no better place to sleep than behind a church?"

"Yessir."

"Damn good thing you said, 'Yes sir,' boy. This here your car?"

Early again, with unusual politeness. "No sir. It belongs to somebody else."

"So you ain't out here by yo' self? That it?" a new voice said.

"No sir."

"No sir? You telling us you out here by yo' self but that that's somebody else's car. You know what I think, boys? This here nigger's goddamn lying. We seen cars out here at night, more 'n one. Ain't that right, boy? Bo, I think the boy's lying."

This was a different voice, distinct, one I'd heard but couldn't immediately place.

Shit!" Sharon hissed. She was hanging onto me, breathing into my ear. "They've seen our cars here. They're coming in here looking for us. How many are there?"

"At least four, I think. Maybe five. That last one sounded familiar."

"Who—"

"Shhhh."

"Well, if he is, we can sure 'nough find out now, cain't we, boy?"

There was an utter complete silence.

Nothing from Early.

"That's five," I said. "That last was a different voice."

"Damn that Early," she said. "He should have run with us."

"You got the key, boy?"

Nothing.

"Oh no," Sharon murmured.

"What?" I said.

"I've got the keys in my pocket," she said.

"I say, you got the key, boy? I'm talking to you, boy."

Nothing.

A loud slap rang through the trees.

"When I talk to you, boy, you answer me. Unnerstand?"

A faint murmur. "I ain't got the key. I lost it. That's why I'm sleeping here."

"Good for him," Sharon said.

"Let's hope," I said.

"Search him, Bo. He's lying. He's got the key." That voice again.

Sharon whispered, "God, Sam, what do we do?" She was clinging to me like I was a raft in a stormy sea, only I was not the raft. I was the stormy sea.

"In a minute, we need to start moving," I said. "Circle back toward the road. There's a house about a half a mile away."

"And leave Early?"

"We don't have a choice. He told them it was somebody else's car. When they don't find the key on him, they may come in here looking for us. You know the SNCC number in Greenwood?"

"Yes. We had to memorize it in training."

"Listen," I said.

"He ain't got it, Top," a voice said.

"My God!" I breathed.

"What?" she said.

"That's one of my church members. At Redbone. It's not far from here. Shhh. Listen."

"We got to solve this here car problem," Hunsucker said. "I think there's more of 'em out there in the woods. We don't need no witnesses."

Discussion. Unintelligible muttering and mumbling.

"Sam, they're going to kill him," Sharon said. "We've got to do something."

"Give me the keys to the car," I said.

"What?"

"The keys."

"Why?" she whispered, almost too loud.

"Just do it. I'll tell you later."

"No. Tell me now."

Our whispers were flying back and forth.

"We're going to start moving to the right," I said. "If you go straight, you'll hit the road about a hundred yards off, maybe sooner."

"Me? By myself?"

"I'm going part of the way with you, but one of us has to stay. It needs to be me. That's why I need the keys."

"I still don't understand why."

"In case they take off with Early, I can follow. You get to that house, call SNCC, then wait for me at the house. I'll get to you as soon as I can. Now, let's start moving, slowly, to the right, toward the road. Put your heels down first."

"This is awfully risky," she said. "They might hear us."

"The rain's softened things up. Just move slowly. We need to stay where we can hear them so we'll know what's going on. They may just knock him around and leave."

"I can't believe you're taking this chance."

"It's the only one we have. Remember, heels down first."

"Wait!" she said. "Listen!"

"Tell you what, boy. Let's walk over to that car and just see if them keys might just be there. Whatta ya say?"

Early was silent. If he said anything, we couldn't hear. We heard sounds of scuffling, then another slap and a muffled whack like a blow to the head with a hard object.

"When I say git, boy, I mean git. Move, goddamn it. Hell fire, they work around mules so damn long they act just like 'em."

Through unfamiliar dark, Sharon and I began moving toward the road in an arc that took us closer to the church. We could see the flashlights and shadows and hear movement and some conversation, but nothing was clear. We tried to move quickly, when they were moving. We reached the point where we needed to separate. If we went further, the remnant of the north wall would cut off my field of vision. We were in a stand of large timber where there were fewer obstructions from underbrush and shrubbery, which meant less protection, but the trunks were large enough to hide us. I was behind one, Sharon behind another. I motioned to her to go on. She waved me off, but I motioned again and whispered, "It's now or never." She slid off through the trees and I watched her disappear into the dark foliage. I prayed she would make it. It might be our only hope. I knew whites lived at the house, the lady who brought us well water.

I leaned close to the tree, pressed my face against the wet bark, watched and listened. Just ahead, near the corner of the church, I could see the car in a small clearing. It listed slightly and moonlight reflected off its top and windshield. Through a tapestry of shadows, bulky silhouettes lurched, pushing and prodding a small crouched figure. They moved behind pools of light that jumped along the ground before them; then they emerged into the small clearing and I saw the tottering white hoods and draped sheets. I turned away, pressed my back against the tree and prayed my lungs would not explode.

So much we are told as children we never choose to believe. It is just cast upon us and we innocently accept. Goblins and ghosts and buggerbears. Ghouls and witches at Halloween and the chicken-foot woman who prowls when the moon is full. For these, we ask our parents to leave a crack in the door and the bathroom light on. Then we grow up and listen and read instead of different tales of horror and terror, of hooded nightriders in white robes marauding the countryside, of homes torched and cars bombed and men shot and children wrapped in gin fans and thrown into rivers and we sleep sound as rocks in the darkest rooms, whether the moon is full or not. Pressed against that tree, I became a child once more. I knew I'd never sleep soundly again.

I listened as the hooded men rummaged through the old car, shouting obscenities at Early, hitting him I was sure by the sounds of padded swats and blows and groans. I said prayers that Sharon would hurry and make it safely and that there'd be a phone at the house. I thumbed the keys in my pocket as though they were a talisman. I petitioned God, played all the odds, pulled out all the spiritual stops. I thought of jumping out, yelling and letting them chase me. I might manage better in a chase than they in their cumbersome robes and hoods. That would give Early a chance to run. I thought of striking out for the road in hopes of flagging down a car or truck. No thought was good, no prayer enough. All I could do was wait.

"Must've been right about that key," a voice said.

"Naw. Ain't no nigger gonna tell the truth," said another.

"Shitfire! Lying or not there ain't no goddamn key. Let's get on with it. You bring the stuff, Bo?"

"Sure 'nough, Top. In the back of yore truck."

"That's good. Y'all go on. I'll take care of this place and catch up."

Hunsucker, again I thought.

"Same place?"

"Same place. Tie up the boy first and put him in the truck."

"What you gonna do with me?" said Early. His voice was rising and breaking, filled with fright.

"That's for us to know and you to find out, boy," cackled one.

"I ain't done nothing to you."

"Nothin' but you and your white lib'rals comin' in here and messin' up our way of life," said Hunsucker. I knew now for sure. The voice, the words, were unmistakable. "Now just shut up and do as they tell you and everthing's gonna be hunkydoory. You hear?"

Hunkydoory. Hunsucker. I held my breath. It seemed all time had stopped and I was bleeding to death, blood running out of me from some hidden wound and there was nothing to check the flow. I was just bleeding away and still afraid to look. I could only guess what was happening by what I could hear. The sounds of scuffling, blows and groans moved away from me up the slope toward the church. Sharon would have had time to reach the road, maybe the house.

I peeked around the tree and saw the tromping hooded group as they turned the corner into the side yard where the lumber and supplies were stacked. A few minutes passed. I could hear only scraps of conversation and guessed they were tying him up. Then doors slammed. One … two … three … four I counted. A motor started. Lights hit the trees, swung across them and vanished. I held my breath. They headed south, away from Sharon.

Only one vehicle pulled out. Hunsucker's truck was still there. I thought of the keys in my pocket, the car, of Early on his way to his death, of Sharon no telling where. My brain was telegraphing, trying to sort out a plan, my heart and lungs working against it. If they would just work together, I thought, maybe I could do something. I crouched down and pushed off from the tree into the surrounding shrubbery and began moving toward the car, feeling my way along the ground with my hands. I heard a tailgate clang then some racket, like Hunsucker was rummaging for something in the bed of the pickup. I moved quickly with the noise. The racket stopped, and I stopped.

The north wall of the church was to my right, near me. I could see both window portals. If I could make it to one, I could glimpse action in the side yard through the window portals in the opposite wall. I moved quietly across the grass until I was against the wall beneath the window near the back and closest to the car. Hugging the wall, I rose slowly. At first, I saw very little, just the other wall, its two windows, the rear wall to my left and the open front to my right. Through the two windows, I could see the stacked lumber, the truck parked beside it. There was a faint sound, like something being threshed or sloshed, I wasn't sure.

Through the left window, a dim amber light shone on the lumber. It came from a flashlight I saw propped on Hunsucker's truck fender. He emerged into the window from the other side of the stacked lumber. He was moving his arms high and wide like the Reaper of Death swinging his scythe. Then I saw the gas can in his hands. That was the reason they had come, to destroy the supplies.

I'm not sure what came over me, a sudden hate, loathing. I am sure of what left me, as though sucked away: fear. I had no thoughts of escape to safety. Every thought—of Early, of Sharon, the church—said stay. Every cell, every nerve within me lasered on Hunsucker.

He stopped a moment and set the can on the ground. I had a good view of him and hoped he didn't move. He looked around and hiked his robe and with a retarded groping motion whisked something from his hip pocket.

Is he going to strike the match before I can distract him? I thought.

He lifted his hood with a hand, leaned back and tilted a bottle to his lips. He took several long gulps, coughed, ran a long sleeve of robe across his mouth, screwed the cap back on the bottle and returned it his hip pocket. He picked up the gas can and moved to the stack of shingles and began circling it. He put the can down again, hiked his robe and whipped the bottle from his hip pocket again. He took more long swigs and put the bottle back but kept his robe hiked and pulled something from his waist. His back was to me. The rays of flashlight from the truck fender were dim, but the movements of his hand, the way it flourished in the meager light left little doubt.

What I saw next on my right struck raw terror. Sharon coming out of the woods near the road, her hair matted and stringy, her soaked clothes hanging on her. She was supposed to wait for me at the house. What the hell is she doing coming back? She thinks they've left, doesn't know Hunsucker's still there, those thoughts sailing through my head as she turned the corner of the church and left my view. She was entering the side yard. Another chill ran through me.

Hunsucker suddenly wheeled with the gun. "Stop right there, whoever you are, or I'll blow your head off," he shouted, his hood teetering with the quick turn.

I couldn't see her or hear her. I could only see Hunsucker. He didn't move.

"Git the hell over here," he said waving the gun.

Through the right window, I saw her again. She was walking slowly, staying close to the wall, her eyes on Hunsucker. *That's good. She's got to know I'm here.* I thought of what was in the car or on the ground around me, anything heavy I could lift.

"I thought so," Hunsucker said. "The boy was lying to us. You one of them other niggers."

She kept moving, the gun moved with her, then I couldn't see her again. *Keep moving*, I was thinking. *Keep him coming with you.* My hand hit something that moved on the window ledge. A loose brick. I gripped it firmly with one hand and began hurriedly working it.

"Pretty little thing for a nigger girl," Hunsucker said derisively. "Wonder what you got under them tight blue jeans," he snickered..

I couldn't believe what I was hearing. You damn bigot, I shouted loudly inside my head. A directed rage swelled within me. Sharon was so calm. She kept coming in and out of my view until I could see both of them through the other portal. Hunsucker had moved closer to her, in my direction, unaware of who was leading whom. The brick was almost free. I worked the next one and it broke loose. *Make him come to me*, I was thinking as I looked back through the window, breathing air that was pumped by a heart not my own.

"Maybe you got some car keys in one of them jeans pockets, huh? What you say let's take a look, girl? Pretty little nigger girl. What you say?"

He stepped toward her and she finally spoke. "I don't have any car keys. That's not my car. And don't call me nigger again."

Hunsucker stopped and swayed. "Oh, oh, what we got here? A smart little pretty colored girl. I think maybe we just need to find out. Pull down them blue jeans, hon, and throw 'em over here."

Sharon stood motionless, glacial eyes, livid face, defiant.

Hunsucker took a step toward her. "Now! I say. You hear me pretty little thing? I mean right goddamn now."

Sharon didn't move.

I slipped closer to the corner of the wall and hurled a brick at the car. A dull clunk echoed through the night air and woods and I jumped back into the shadow of the wall.

"Goddamn! What was that?" shouted Hunsucker. "Maybe you got a friend, huh, girlie? Whataya say we go see?"

I could still see him shambling back to the truck to retrieve the flashlight. He shined it on Sharon. Her back was to me, but I could imagine what he saw on her face: a glare of pure hate.

"Now, let's us just walk pretty little thing down to that there car and see if you got a friend and let 'em know if they don't come out, I'm gonna shoot yore pretty little blue jeans off your pretty little colored ass."

Both left my vision. Footsteps stomped the sodden ground then padded through the grass. I could hear his breathing and grunting and knew they were getting closer to me and the car. My breathing locked, my back imprinted on the brick wall, I waited.

I waited.

I waited.

Past the dark line of the wall, Sharon came into view, Hunsucker stumbling behind, the gun at her back. He must've moved closer to her when I couldn't see them. He was a doddering shape mumbling to itself, the gun unsteady in his hand. I was concerned the gun might go off, but knew I must wait. "Not yet," I whispered to myself, "Not yet," as I watched the two move closer to the car.

Hunsucker shambled further toward the car, stopped a few yards from it, bent over like a mechanical dunce, and shouted. "All right, som bitch. Come out. I know you there."

His speech was slurred and he moved closer to the car, one-stepping as though it was a crouched beast that might spring on him. Then he was there, his gun pointed back toward Sharon, his head bobbing around the windows.

For the first time, I realized there was more to his funny movements than booze. It had eyes like clean bullet holes but the hood blocked his peripheral vision. He bent over again.

"Now!" I whispered, kicked off from the wall and lunged toward him.

18

When I came to, all I could hear were cicadas and whippoorwills. I felt hands on my forehead, opened my eyes and saw Sharon's face.

"Are you all right?" she said, "Are you all right?" her eyes wild with fright.

I dug my elbows into the ground and pushed up. I felt something heavy, like a log, lying across my legs pinning them down. It was Hunsucker's leg. Sharon lifted it so I could twist free. I pulled myself up by the car door handle. Sweat was running into the corners of my eyes and I wiped them with the heels of my hands.

"I'm okay," I finally managed. "But he's not."

"He's not moving," she panted. She knelt and lifted his wrist, felt his pulse. "He's dead. Where's Early?"

"They took him. It's not good. But it'll be worse if we don't get this one out of here."

"Oh God, no!" she panicked. "They're going to kill Early."

"Did you get help?" I said.

"No. No one was at home. That's why I came right back."

"It's just as well. We don't need anybody else here."

"What'll we do?" she said exasperated.

"Get us and this body out of here and get to a phone."

I ran to the truck and retrieved the flashlight. The beam was weak but bloomed brighter when I shook it. I shined it first on my shirt and jeans and saw large, wet blood stains. I ran back to the car and Sharon and turned the flashlight on Hunsucker whose blood turned darker on the sheet that shone fluorescent beneath the moonlight. The lower part of his face and eyes were visible beneath the hood that had crawled upward with the impact of the clubbing. The light on his open eyes gave them a strange, glassy luster. His lips were slightly curled, as if in a final jeer, his teeth clenched. *You not one of them radicals.* A thick, smooth line of blood ran from his temple across his cheek to his neck where it forked into separate streams and ran under the collar of his robe. In the soft glare of the light, it looked like a stream of molten wax frozen in place.

"For God's sake, quit shining the light on him," she said. "Let's go before someone comes."

"We've got to clean up, not leave evidence." A few feet to the left of Hunsucker's head I shined the light and saw the brick lying in the grass where it had rolled from my hand. A few more feet from that, the other brick I'd thrown. I handed her the flashlight. "Shine it down there. This won't take long." In the weakening glow of the beam, I smashed the bricks against each other and peppered the woods with the sticky shards, slinging them in every direction. The remaining chips and fragments I ground into the grass and rain-softened soil with my heel. I was working fast. The cicadas had stopped, then they took up again. Somewhere in the distance the howling of a hound.

"Sam, we've got to go."

I bent over Hunsucker, assessing how to move him.

"Why not put the body in his truck and drive it somewhere?" she said. "Surely, he's got his keys on him."

The sound of an approaching motor froze us. We looked at each other then the woods. Lights swept across the trees. A car sped past.

"We can't put him in the truck," I said. "Somebody might pass and see us."

"Then I'll drive the truck down here," she said.

"No. They could trace the truck faster. Let's put him in the trunk of this car and get out of here. We can dump him somewhere. They've done it enough to your people," I said.

We each gripped a booted foot and pulled him around to the back of the car. I rummaged in my pockets for the keys. At first, the key wouldn't turn, then the trunk finally popped open. I placed the flashlight in the angle of the raised lid. I grabbed one arm and she took the other. The wide sleeves of the sheet fell away revealing chunky hairy arms, the tattoo of a confederate flag on one and a cross and bones on the other, something I would ponder later, the kinship between the two. We heaved and lifted him up. He was heavier than anything I'd ever lifted. It took all my strength, from my wrist to my shoulder, my back to my thighs, but adrenalin was pumping, motivation working against laws of gravity and physics.

We got his head onto the rim of the trunk, then lifted, pushed harder and muscled his shoulders in. I pulled his robe up over his waist and grabbed his belt, told Sharon to do the same, and we hoisted and rolled him headfirst into the oil-smelling trunk, folding and tucking his legs in behind. The robe was still up around his waist, and I saw the bottle.

"Did you touch that bottle with your hands when you were getting him in?" I said.

"No. That was on your side."

"Better not take any chances." I slipped the bottle from his hip pocket. We were ready to leave.

"Wait. Look around. Make sure we're not leaving anything that would identify us," she said.

With the fading flashlight, we scoured the ground. His bottle was under my belt. Everything else we had brought was in the car.

"What about the flashlight?" she said.

"We'll take it with us. We'll need it. Let's go. It'll recharge some," I said and handed the keys to her. "You've driven this trap, I haven't."

She started the car and put the gears in reverse. The tires whined briefly in the wet grass, then caught traction and carried us up the slope and into the side yard. She stopped, wrenched the wheel to the right, backed again until we were pointed toward the road, then straightened the wheel. Hunsucker's truck and the supply stacks were on our right. The can was still on the ground where he'd left it, between the lumber and shingles and the church. In both directions, the road was dark and lifeless.

"Should we get anything else?" she said.

"No. Let's get the hell out of here."

"Which way do we go?"

"Shit," I exclaimed.

"What!"

"If we go south, that's the direction they took Early. But that's where my car is. North takes us toward Acona and Blackhawk where I've got churches and people know me. How much gas you got?"

"Enough."

My adrenaline and brain connected. For once they were working together. "Good. Go south. I've got an idea."

"What?"

"Just go, dammit. I'll tell you on the road. And for God's sake, don't speed. Wait!"

I opened the door and ran toward the stack of concrete blocks beside the lumber. I picked up two and lugged them back, flung them in the back seat, and ran back for two more.

"What are those for?" she said.

"I'll tell you later. They might come in handy."

She let off the clutch and we lurched forward and bounced onto the gravel road. She waited a few seconds before turning on the headlights. I checked my watch. Half past ten. I explained the plan to her while she drove and watched the rear as I talked. She would slow down and let me out at the small store where my car was parked. There was no pay phone at the store, so she would keep going toward Tchula where she could call the Greenwood SNCC headquarters and tell them about Early. They could alert the Feds. I would drive back in the direction we had come, cut across between Blackhawk and Coila, make a wide half-circle and meet her south of Cruger at the Morgan Brake turnoff, our former meeting spot.

She couldn't think of a better plan and agreed.

The implications of Early's kidnapping were beginning to sink in. She was wiping tears with one hand and driving with the other. Beneath the tough exterior, a fragile core was unraveling. Her body shook and trembled. She pounded the wheel with her fist, cursing God that He could allow this to happen. I tried to calm her and kissed her on the cheek before sliding out the door as she slowed in front of the store.

I drove as planned. The church was a shapeless ruin in the light of the moon. Hunsucker's truck was still there. I accelerated on the turn and sped northward. There was no traffic, and I breathed easier as I made the turn north of Blackhawk and headed toward Greenwood. The road ran in a northwesterly direction, veered sharply south where it descended into the Delta and continued southward, contouring the bluffs.

Thoughts came like the myriad moths and night bugs whirling aimless out of the thick night pocking the windshield. I was concerned about my clothes and how I would dispose of them, about what I would say if stopped, or what I would do if the front tire blew as Ivy Lee had warned. I drove on in the night, the agonizing images of arrest, jail and execution on my mind and the grief of losing all I had ever owned in my life if I were caught. And the alternate disquieting thoughts if I pulled it off, facing myself and my churches, preaching to them as if nothing had happened, especially at Redbone. I'd have to greet them with a false rectitude. I'd have to pray for one of their own. Guilt became a hot wind whipping through the windows.

Sharon was there at the turnoff spot. Another car was coming so I drove a distance down the road and turned around. The way was clear on the second pass and I turned in beside her. Her head was slumped over the wheel. She raised as I turned off the lights. I left my motor running and walked to her side of the car. Through the lowered window, she looked like another person, someone aged beyond her years.

"Did you call headquarters?" I said.

"Yes."

"What did they say?"

"They were shocked. Stokely wasn't in, but the girl who answered said they would get word out as soon as possible. A carload is heading now toward the vicinity where Early was abducted."

"Did you tell them anything else?" I said.

"No, stupid."

"Sorry, I just—"

"Don't apologize. We've got to do something fast."

"We can't get rid of him here," I said. "That logging trail only goes about fifty yards or so. Hunters or dogs would find him in a matter of days."

"I know, but where? My brain is numb. I can't think."

"Follow me," I said.

"Where?"

"Never mind. Just follow me."

From Greenwood, the Yazoo River ran south through Belzoni, which was almost due west. I knew, too, there was a county road from Tchula to Swifttown, just north of Belzoni. I'd seen the marker on previous trips back and forth. We drove south to Tchula. I kept checking my rearview to make sure she was behind me. Traffic was sparse, a car or pickup every few miles. Except for a gas station where a lone attendant sat leaning against a wall in a cane-back chair, late night Tchula was empty. Streetlamps, like globed moons, hung over its lone dark streets.

We turned west onto the county road. Potholes and the warped aging of the old road rocked the car. Her lights bounced behind me. The flat land was dark except the images our headlights clipped from it. An occasional pair of eyes flared then died. *A deer maybe, or fox,* I thought after the initial fright passed. We didn't need both cars and I slowed, hoping to see a place where we could leave mine. We were about five miles out of Tchula. Still, no traffic. I saw a wide spot on the roadside, pulled over and turned off my lights. She pulled in behind me. I got out, locked my car, ran back and got in with her.

"Would you please tell me what the hell we're doing," she said.

"We're going to throw him in the river."

"God bless, Sam. We can't do that. He'll just float right back up. And if anyone saw these cars, it's all over."

"We're going to be careful, and no one's going to see us. And he won't float back up for a long time, maybe never, not with four concrete blocks holding him down."

"You gotta be crazy. We don't have anything to tie him to the blocks with."

"There was a towing chain in the trunk. I saw it when we were putting him in. This old trap has probably broken down a time or two."

She put the car in gear and guided us back onto the road. For a mile or so, we drove through open cotton fields. Then I saw it, a single lane, dirt road on the left. I told her to turn. There was still nothing but cotton on either side, as high almost as the car, sweeping by like a continuous hedge, no end in sight and no turnaround. The smell of defoliant was strong. I sensed we'd taken a wrong turn and were entrapped in a maze. We both sensed it.

"Sam, this is really crazy. There's no way out of here. We should stop and back up."

"Just a little farther. We're in a cotton field. There has to be a turn row or exit somewhere."

The road was narrowing, cotton swishing along the sides of the car. She was exasperated and about to stop when the road T-boned with another.

She stopped in the intersection. "What now?"

"This is it," I said. "Let's rig him up here. Maybe there's enough power left in the flashlight."

We got out. The sky was clear, the moon high, dark shapes of cotton and trees surrounded us. Sharon shook the light and the beam burned brighter. She held it while I opened the trunk. A strange and noxious odor hit us when we raised the lid and both of us let out audible breaths. The body was in a fetal curl on top of the chain, and I had to rock it back and forth to free the tangled linkage. It was a single tow chain with a large hook at one end.

"You're going to chain him up here with the blocks?" Sharon said.

"Don't know anyway else to do it. It's the same thing they did to Emmit Till, only with a gin fan. It would take too long at the river and I'm afraid somebody might come along. We can throw him in when we get there and high tail it."

I retrieved the blocks from the back seat. The task was more difficult than I'd imagined. The blocks were heavy and bulky, no guarantee they'd stay attached once he hit the river. I had thought about those problems on the way and almost decided burying him was better, but we were here and needed to do something right away.

Sharon held the dying light that jiggled with her tremors as I threaded the chain through the blocks and began wrapping him, pulling tightly each loop around Hunsucker's body as it lay in the trunk. The chain was long and made several revolutions. With frightening efficiency, I looped it back and made two half-hitches, a knot I'd learned in Boy Scouts. The blocks rested unevenly on top of him and would probably sag when we took him out, but they would hold. They had to.

"Now, just how do we get the car out of here?" she said. "There's not room to turn around."

"Pull straight ahead."

"But there's cotton straight ahead."

"Run over it, then back onto the other road."

We bumped over a row, cotton bolls knocking on the undercarriage and along the side of the car, backed up, came forward, backed again, turned and headed out.

"After all that we should've just buried him right there," she grunted. "Or just thrown him out. They might've found him in a year."

"They would've found him at cotton picking time," I said.

No one laughed.

The road was clear as we entered it and turned west again. Nothing was said as we approached an old iron trestle bridge. I knew it had to span the Yazoo.

"What do I do here?" she said.

"Just pull to the middle of the bridge. Nothing's coming. This shouldn't take long."

The car clattered slowly onto the bridge's wooden floor. She did as I'd instructed and let it roll to the middle, turned off the lights but kept the motor running. The space between the car and the lip of the bridge was the distance I was sitting from her but it seemed wide as an ocean.

The next minutes passed as hours. In our rush to get the body out of the trunk, we were not thinking about physics or leverage. We grappled and pulled at cloth and material that slipped and tore flimsily through our hands, but nothing moved. I told her to get his feet. I managed to get my hands under his armpits, and we rolled him up and over the bumper, giving each other stricken looks when body, blocks and chain hit the bridge and the loud crash reverberated up and down the moonlit river.

The chain had loosened and I pulled the crisscrossed configurations tighter until they squeezed the body. I looped and re-looped the ends, securing the hook snugly under his belt so the blocks aligned along Hunsucker's hips like huge cogs.

"You've got to pull them tighter," Sharon said.

"I'm pulling them tight as I can."

"Sam, this is not going to work. We should've buried him."

"Too late for that. You get his feet again. I'll get his arms."

Like farm children trying to move a dead hog, we half-dragged, half-rolled Hunsucker's body across the bridge, the echo of the blocks clunking on the planking, until we finally had him poised on the edge. A shove completed the act.

The splash was a thunderous concussion, that of a monstrous boulder plunging suddenly into quiet, undisturbed water. The river quickly recovered its rhythm. Moon-reflected curls and eddys resumed their southward glide, lapping softly along the dark banks where nothing else moved at midnight. Against that quiet, the whiskey bottle made a dimpled *plop* into the water below. I'd removed the cap to ensure it would sink.

We stood listening for any other noises.

The silence was breathless.

That funeral was over.

As we drove away, I recalled a worship service my mother dragged me to one July midnight at a small church north of New Albany. She didn't say why we were going, though I would understand years later. A preacher dressed up like a devil carrying a pail with a lantern tromped among the congregation, yanked the red light up in my face and cried out, "The devil walks at midnight. Repent or burn in hell fire." I felt the devil, the vibrations of his heavy feet, tromping on that bridge that midnight.

19

The smell of defoliant, insecticide and dust sucked through the car's open windows. Oil and exhaust fumes wafted upward through a hole in the floor. But the strongest smell was another. Blood blotted the front of my shirt and tops of my jeans. The sickly sight and odor drew me closer to the window. Insects swept from the fringes of the dark. Sounds seemed magnified. The uneven ricking of the motor and the creak and rattle of the car's joints were all we could hear. Along the road's shoulder, eyes of curs and bobcats burned and died away. A red fox, a *tchula,* wheeled in the edge of light, then dissolved into the dark. Bright moonlight streaked along the high wires.

"Remember, get rid of your clothes," Sharon said. "You've got blood all over you. Burn them if you can and scatter the ashes."

"What will you tell them?" I said.

"Just what happened, that Early and I were together at the church. The nightriders came. They took him, but I managed to escape into the woods." She was wiping back tears again.

"And the car?"

"I waited in the woods. When I thought everyone was gone, I snuck in and floorboarded myself out of there."

"But the truck—"

"I didn't look to check on any truck," she said, her voice shaking.

"What about where you were between the time you called and when you checked in?"

"I was in a daze, lost. I got turned around."

"What if the men recognized the car or got the tag number?"

"So what. Everybody's gonna know the car was there." She gave me a long painful look.

Then it hit me. "I'm sorry. I didn't mean for this to put you—"

"Don't worry," she said angrily. "They have Early to answer for."

We discussed cover-ups and strategies. I gave her two quarters for the all-night car wash in Tchula. I told her to clean the trunk but not too clean, just get rid of the blood. It needed to look like a normal used car trunk. She managed a "thanks" and squeezed my hand and continued holding it as we neared the spot where I had parked.

It was early morning and still dark, but we knew not to linger long, just enough for a hug, a kiss and a covenant for life.

I drove back to Mount Pleasant in a daze. My mouth was dry, my legs rubbery on the clutch and accelerator. My arms felt lighter than air, as though they'd levitate if I let go of the wheel. I imagined how boxers might feel after fifteen rounds. *Uncle Giles, did you ever kill a man?* That was in a war. Any man he killed would have been a soldier. This was war, too, I reasoned. But the man I killed was no soldier. He was scum, wretched of the earth, a roach I'd step on. What I did was necessary. We both did what was necessary. The reasons didn't matter. Both of us were wrong. We both felt shame. You can't get around the Ten Commandments. You can't get around, "Thou shalt not kill."

In that lightless dawn, only the streetlights hinted of life as I drove into Mount Pleasant. I turned off the headlights and coasted into the parsonage drive. Before unlocking the side house door, I retrieved a can of gasoline from the storage closet in the garage and set it beside the door stoop. Once inside the house, I quickly removed my clothes, except for my underwear. I grabbed a flashlight that always sat on the kitchen counter and took the bloodied discards behind the house and doused them with gasoline. No one, I thought, would see me in my underwear, and if they did would probably think they were pajama bottoms.

I moved the fifty gallon garbage can to the back of the house, the only safe place to burn the clothes. The backyard was deep and surrounded by bushy privet hedges. I struck a match and dropped it. Flames immediately shot upward. In a short while, the job was done, but I was almost asleep in the grass. I dumped the fluffy ashes onto a newspaper, balled it up, then scattered the ashes across the back of the yard near the hedges and dropped the newspaper into the fifty-gallon can. With the flashlight, I re-checked my car for bloodstains.

I saw none. But wait, the steering wheel. I wiped it thoroughly with wet paper napkins that showed pink under the faint glow of the flashlight. I did the same with the interior, anything I might have touched and threw the rags into the fifty-gallon can where low flames were still visible. I thought of Sharon and hoped she was doing the same.

I worried about the car trunk. She needed to clean up the blood, but not much more. A spic and span trunk would be a flashing arrow. I thought and rethought, traced and retraced, what I might have left undone, what trail not covered, stone left unturned. My mind fought against my body to stay awake just a little longer, just to make sure. I filled the molded bathtub and felt the stings of briar scratches as I slipped into the warm water. I scrubbed my hands and arms and face until my skin burned raw and watched as pinkish rivulets trailed off into the sudsy water.

I got out of the tub and stood there looking around with uncertainty. What had I forgotten? In murder mysteries, one thing is usually forgotten. My eyes fell on the washcloth. With a pair of scissors, I cut it into tiny pieces and flushed them down the commode then knelt and lowered my head. A sickness lurched in my stomach. My body wretched and spewed into the bowl. The sour taste followed me into sleep and dreams where hollow-eyed phantoms kept uncovering my tracks.

Years afterward, in nightmares vivid as documentary footage, I was reminded what I had done. What, in those chilling moments, I had been.

20

When I attempt to recall them, the last days of July sloughed by like a blur. Dawns and dusks seemed to cancel each other. At times, I was uncertain where reality ended and illusion began, and vice-versa. I didn't know whether time was going backwards or forwards or if I was even moving with it. I didn't know if I was waking from a nightmare or living one. My eyelids felt like they were on springs. At night, my eyes would approach sleep, but I rarely fell asleep. The wasteland of sleepless nights had its opposite daytime counterpart. I was overcome with narcoleptic ambushes. Everywhere I went, an air of misery followed me. Spiritually, I felt the depth of my sins. I felt fragmented, scattered, more solitary than ever. The call to preach I'd once heard had been muted.

I forced myself out of the parsonage and through a minimal routine that included stops at the church where I stayed the mornings and at Ivy Lee's to buy a newspaper. I jumped when the telephone rang. Cars slowing in front of the house sent me running to ensure the doors were locked. Seeing a police officer set off alarms in my head I thought surely the whole world could hear. The closest to a tranquilizer was cool water running over my face. I drank my meals—Campbell's soup, milkshakes and tomato juice. Nothing solid could pass through my throat. Often, the knot there was so oppressive I had trouble breathing.

I sought refuge in my oldest memories, those untouched by anything recent. Those long ago memories—riding alone with Giles, fishing with my grandparents, playing centerfield in Little League Baseball, hitting a home run—the ones that were always kind, generous and infused with some comfort, even if thin and fleeting.

Sharon and I spoke daily by phone. She kept me abreast of events and told of her agonizing interviews with the sheriff's department and Highway Patrol, how they had accused her of concocting the story of Early's abduction, that it was a conspiracy to draw media attention to the church burning, another communist plot by campus radicals. "Professional troublemakers" Senator Stennis had called them from the U. S. Senate floor.

She took verbal abuse that ran the scale of cruelty but, unlike so many others, she was not beaten. The FBI agents were kinder, but said they could not intervene, only take information and pass it on. She was certain their presence had been a deterrent, as it had with the SNCC volunteers in the hospital. Yet everyone was stunned at their refusal to take any action— anywhere in the state. They were watchful bystanders, nothing more. This was our government, the one that guaranteed our freedoms, the one that protected us. To everyone, she told the same story. She gave details no one could invent.

On Thursday, three days after the incident, the headline in the local paper read TOP HUNSUCKER MISSING. No other first name was given, as though "Top" said it all. I could only think *Bottom, Low-down.* There was no picture. Two paragraphs gave his description and address and sent shocks to my nerves. "He was last seen at Barber's Grocery in the Redbone community. His empty pickup truck was found at the burned C. M. E. Bethel Church. Authorities are investigating." A telephone number was provided for anyone having knowledge of his whereabouts could call.

The same day, Sharon was called back to the sheriff's department for more questioning. She stuck with her story and said she barely remembered seeing the truck when she left. For this, a deputy slapped her. He said she was lying and protecting the ringleaders of the conspiracy. He would have hit her again, she said, if two FBI agents had not been present in the small room. Officers were in the process of locking her up when one of the agents reminded them, only after repeated urging from SNCC core leaders, that she was being denied her civil rights and due process. She was released but told not to leave the county. She was a suspect in the disappearance of a white male named Top Hunsucker.

That following Sunday, I had to face my churches and gave thanks Redbone was not on the rotation. I would have to face that congregation the following Sunday but, for the time being, I had a reprieve. My mind was in no shape to prepare a sermon, so I dipped into my meager collection and chose something I'd delivered in homiletics class in seminary.

I didn't preach my sermon; I read it. My prayers were short, perfunctory. The biggest problem I encountered was sitting on the dais during the silent interludes and finding new places to look. Most of the time, I looked down pretending I was in prayer. Before the service and after, people gathered in their customary places and talked the usual—of crops, the heat, the fall revival. An occasional word was said about Top Hunsucker. "He was just pullin' another 'un on his folks," an older man remarked. Hunsucker never married and lived with his parents.

Later that night, I called Sharon and suggested we see each other. Monday was my day off, and we could drive to Jackson in the morning and find refuge at Tougaloo. It was best we not be seen together for a while, she said, even among her own. I painfully agreed, despite my feeling of uneasiness and rejection. Still, I was not satisfied.

"Is that all? Shar, is there something you're not telling me?" I said trying to throttle a rising panic in my throat, my voice.

"We just don't need to see each other."

"I don't understand. I thought—"

"Sam. This is not about understanding." Her voice had hardened. "Regardless of what happened to Early, or to that man, we could never—"

"We could—"

"We could never be together. There is too much against us. I care deeply for you and will eternally love you. Our situation is more painful to me than I can put into words."

Not until a generation later would I learn the reality of that pain, the depth of her care. Mine had plummeted to self-pity and self-contempt. I grasped at the voice I was losing, at the life that was leaving me. She was on another level.

"But what about our commitment?" I said, a tremor in my voice.

"It's still there, as strong as ever. But we cannot be lovers." She spoke calmly and with unabridged completeness. The air around me crystallized. The muscles in my body twisted like wires. I breathed needles. The receiver was hot against my ear. In those moments, I felt I was being cut to pieces by tenderness for there was no harshness in the tone of her tough honesty.

The conversation ended that evening with affection. Words of love, it had been decided, were not realistic.

Choked with a sorrow I had never known, I hung up the receiver, broke down and sobbed.

In the days and months that followed, I withdrew into a wounded silence and moved in a world of private and desperate anxiety. My greatest fear was not the unveiling of my crime, but that something special was gone from my life that would never be replaced. I did not even have a picture of her. I carried her name like a weight, a phantom limb, feeling her by feeling where she no longer existed.

21

Monday, August 3

A week to the day after his abduction, Early's body was found. A black hunter stumbled across it in a wooded area in the next county. I learned of the tragedy in the worst of places. The men at Ivy Lee's were talking more than usual as I walked over for my daily mid-morning Coke and newspaper. I caught scattered words. Nigger. Body. Burned. I passed up the Coke, slapped a dime on Ivy Lee's oily counter and picked up a copy of the Greenwood paper.

Back at the parsonage, tears rolled down my face as I read the account. He'd been beaten and shot several times. According to the report, "The burning of the body may have been a cover-up, but for what, the FBI does not know or is not saying. They will continue investigating." The article concluded that he had been working with SNCC volunteers rebuilding the Bethel C. M. E. Church. I called Sharon, and we wept together. She said his murder had demoralized the workers, but that they were still moving ahead with the rebuilding of the church. I couldn't take my mind off how he died and remembered how he had almost died as an infant in a fire set by a racist.

I fell on my knees and sobbed in rage.

Several times, Sharon and I commiserated by phone. In voices trembling with tears, we questioned our actions. Why did we run into the woods and not stay? Why did I hesitate, do nothing to distract the hooded thugs? The thought was unnerving as was another: abandonment of a friend to his death. "Greater love hath no man than this, that he lay down his life for his friends." The scripture I knew so well haunted me.

The next evening in an earthen dam two counties removed, beneath a glare of flashlights and the eyes of federal authorities, the bodies of three civil rights workers—James Chaney, Michael Schwerner and Andy Goodman—were discovered. Media attention riveted on Philadelphia, Mississippi, city of "brotherly love."

In our grief, Sharon and I felt a sense of relief. Early's lynching had drawn attention away from Hunsucker's disappearance, and this latest headline was sure to move our victim further down the authorities' agenda.

Our false sense of relief was short-lived. The early morning television news of the following Friday reported that Top Hunsucker's body had been discovered southeast of Swifttown and northeast of Belzoni, just inside Humphreys County. The middle-aged white male was entangled in a white sheet and his skull had been crushed, probably by a large rock. There was no mention of the hood or the chains and concrete blocks. I prayed they were mired in silt and sludge, along with the bottle, at the bottom of the Yazoo River. The reporter went on to say foul play was suspected. Though there were no leads at that point, authorities believed the death was related to a counter-attack against the Ku Klux Klan by radical armed Negroes or white insurgents connected with SNCC or that perennial suspect, the Communists.

A shiver slid along my nerves. I found myself thinking how I thought the authorities might be thinking and a frightful logic took hold. An eye for an eye, a tooth for a tooth. Early lynched. Hunsucker lynched in retaliation. Now Chaney, Schwerner and Goodman. The ultimate quid-pro-quo spiral of violence.

Where would it stop?

22

Saturday, August 8

Two days before I was to return to Atlanta and seminary, Sharon phoned. She was called in again for questioning. The authorities were gentler this time, she said. The FBI and media looking over their shoulders, they were more cautious. She was released. Not because her story was consistent and tight, she said, but because investigators seemed convinced a woman could not have inflicted such massive cranial damage. She overheard one say the coroner at the University Medical Center in Jackson likened it to a head run over by a Mack truck, the worst skull damage he'd ever seen. Had they kept her, I had already decided to turn myself in.

I knew the phone call might be my last time to speak with her before our lives went in different directions. The loneliness that had been rising within me like an unrelenting flood surged. The kind of loneliness that made time seem slower, days longer and clocks tick louder. The kind of loneliness that took on a physical suffocating quality. The kind of loneliness I felt I could reach out and touch.

To distract from my anguish and put some order into the disarray my life had become, I spent most of that day at the parsonage packing. Something about packing always infused me with a sense of hope. I was leaving one place and going to another, departing one that had become suddenly empty and headed toward one with the glimpse of a future.

Mid-afternoon, I was in the back bedroom folding clothes and was startled by three loud knocks at the front door. On shaky legs, I walked to the door and slowly opened it. Two highway patrolmen politely introduced themselves as state investigators and said they needed to ask me some questions. I managed to control my breathing but my heart was pounding my ribs. I needed to keep the patrolmen at the door. The living room was cluttered with boxes and looked like a small disorganized warehouse.

They seemed content to stand on the small porch and ask their questions, which related to my knowledge, as his pastor, of Top Hunsucker. I gave only short answers. Did he ever confide in me about any enemies or any trouble he was in? No. Was I aware of any strange or unusual behavior? No. He was always easy going and mild mannered, I offered. I was tempted to tell them he was a member of the Klan and hated niggers and nigger lovers, but I would be telling them what they already knew, giving them too much information. I was prepared with an answer about my whereabouts that night, but they never asked. They thanked me, tipped their hats and left.

The remainder of the afternoon passed quietly. I raised all the windows, turned on the stereo and played Tchaikovsky, music bold, triumphant, reinforcing. For the first time in days, I was beginning to feel some relief. I had not been arrested.

I returned to packing. Later, at first I didn't hear the knocks. In the raised volume of the stereo they might have been from the orchestra's percussion section. I lowered the volume. A light, hesitant knocking sound came again. Again, someone was at the front door, and again my heartbeat started pounding. I wasn't out of the woods yet.

I opened the door and saw an older man I immediately recognized. He was tall and slightly stooped. The white shirt he was wearing hung from his shoulders and his overall straps sagged. A pair of spectacles protruded from the bib pocket. His face was long, a rough oval cut, and he had a purple fever blister on his lower lip. A hat line across his forehead divided sunburn from a pale, almost hairless, scalp. Holding the brim of his straw hat beneath his chin, he had the expression of a small child sent on a difficult errand.

"Brother Ransom, guess by now you heard 'bout our boy, Top." The words seemed to bubble up through his throat. His glaucous eyes looked tired with deep-circles below them.

The words and the obsequious tone of his voice tripped an alarm, one I'd not expected. After all, I was Hunsucker's pastor. I'd met his parents twice on home visits to see him. He had told me they went to a Baptist church. I forced my eyes into the elderly man's. "Yessir, Mr. Hunsucker. I am very sorry."

"Thank ye kindly. We're God-fearin' folk, Brother Ransom. 'Vengeance is mine, saith the Lord.' Who ever done it'll pay, 'ventually. We just pray for that. But the reason I come. His mama and me want—"

"Excuse me, Mr. Hunsucker. I'll be right back." I left him standing in the doorway turning the brim of his hat in his hands. I knew what was coming and retreated to the bathroom where I could think beyond *who ever done it'll pay*. I downed a glass of water and returned. Beneath a bland stare, his hands were still rotating his hat.

"Sorry, Mr. Hunsucker. I had to use the bathroom."

He blinked he understood and continued. "Well sir, like I was saying, his mama and me want you to bury our boy. He said you was a little too lib'ral and sech, but he liked you."

He liked you. The words overwhelmed me. He would have liked Early, too. That was the insane and painful problem of that fragmented world in that time. No one really knew or trusted anyone. Fear had turned into hate. I hesitated a moment, looked around at the packed boxes and luggage. I wanted him to look, too, pick up the hint. I was leaving. I wouldn't have time. But he stood there, waiting.

"Mr. Hunsucker, I imagine the funeral service will be Tuesday and I'm leaving Monday morning. Brother Allshouse is the senior pastor of the charge, and I know he would be willing to conduct the funeral." I wasn't thinking fast enough to tell him I had never conducted a funeral and that I wouldn't have time to prepare a service in such short notice.

"Well sir. We want you to do it. The fun'ral won't be Tuesday. Hit'll be Monday. We done checked with Brother Allshouse and he said you'd have time. I'll be on my way now. He was our only boy. Alls we want is a Christian fun'ral, and you were his preacher."

He raised his hat with both hands, placed it squarely on his head, adjusted it just right across his forehead and flicked the brim with his finger. "Much obliged, Brother Ransom. Much obliged. 'Spect you out our way soon. Got tables of food," then he turned and limped to his truck that sat idling in the street.

The sky was darkening. Traffic was picking up through the quiet streets. People going home from work, back to simple, undisturbed lives. I felt nauseated and walked to the bedroom and sat on the edge of the bed. A faint clicking pervaded the room. It came from nowhere in particular, but seemed everywhere. The stereo. I never heard the music stop. I went and looked. The needle was stuck in the spidery grooves at the record's glossy core. I lifted the arm, placed it onto its rest and turned off the stereo. If only other things in life could be unstuck so easily. I thought of people everywhere stuck in their ceaseless grooves.

I assessed my approach carefully and placed a call to Brother Allshouse. He was excessively cordial and went on about how he had missed hearing from me. When he stopped to take a breath, I wedged in my reason for calling. He listened and seemed sincere in understanding my situation. A friend of mine, someone I grew up with, was being buried in my hometown, and I felt obligated to be present. His family was expecting me. I didn't tell him that he was black and a civil rights worker and recently found murdered and burned one county removed. Brother Allshouse said he had already spoken with the Hunsucker family, said he was sorry and politely declined. He'd be happy to help any other time but he had an out-of-town trip, plans that could not be changed.

23

Monday, August 10

That early August afternoon was sweltering. Few people stirred outside. Dampness hung in the air; heat shimmered and rose from the macadam road. Mists, like blue smoke, lay along the horizon. The windows were down but the car felt like a sauna. It was that kind of day.

Top Hunsucker's service was simple. A few hymns were sung—*In the Garden; Precious Lord; Higher Ground; Lord, I'm Coming Home.* I followed the ritual from *The Discipline*, glad, for once, the book existed. I read first from the Old, then the New Testament: familiar passages of hope and resurrection, of a Presence. Thankfully, the casket, immediately beneath the pulpit, was closed. I could not look at the family and kept my eyes on the words I sang and read.

For strength, I thought of Early and his funeral occurring at the same time miles to the north in New Albany. The terrible irony that I was burying the man I killed, the same who conspired in Early's murder, did not escape me. For the first time, I began to understand week-long wakes and why Negroes had them. People would leave Early's service feeling they'd really buried someone. "They be for the livin' and not the dead," Giles had once said of funerals. From the scattered memories, that fragment returned to me. We white folks take a couple of days and handful of hours, then linger around for years in bereavement. We give lip service to the Resurrection.

But for the black community, the rising of Christ from the dead was bedrock. Early had already risen. They were celebrating.

* * *

Early's funeral was long over when I arrived in New Albany in the late afternoon. Flowers remained on a mound of red dirt. There was no marker. His family couldn't afford one. I fought the thought of driving by Sharon's house several doors down from Giles' place to see her, and eventually gave in. She would not leave for school until the sixteenth of the month.

I got out, stepped onto the porch and knocked on a screen door that flapped loosely in its frame. There was no answer. Normally, there'd be someone sitting on the porch and kids outside playing. I peeked through a window. The house was dark; it looked deserted. I saw no furniture. I turned to leave, then went back to the door and tried it. Locked.

I got back into the car and drove on up the hill to see Giles. I had seen him eight or nine years ago, that day in the winter rain from inside my house when my mother said he would catch his death. His house looked the same, the big gum tree in front and the small yard that seemed to withdraw from around its roots. Giles and Evie were sitting on the porch framed by wisteria vines, the blooms long gone.

Uncle Giles did you ever kill a man? I needed to talk to someone who'd understand, who'd keep my confessions confidential. I wasn't sure I'd get the chance. Maybe Evie would leave us alone.

Both rose as I pulled into the drive. He was wearing his usual overalls and Evie had on a print dress. In her hand was a homemade cardboard fan, a popsicle stick for a handle. "Haven't seen you in a coon's age," she said. I'd always wondered where that saying came from. How long did coons live? Whatever, for me it seemed a very long time.

We greeted and hugged. Evie pulled another chair from inside onto the porch, and we sat and talked. I brought them up to date about where I was in seminary. I told them about the summer experience with my churches. I told them about the funeral I'd conducted that afternoon, the reason I couldn't attend Early's. I told them it was my first funeral.

Evie did the talking. Giles listened, nodding and grunting approval. Rheumatism and arthritis were mentioned frequently. When I asked about Sharon, Giles remained silent. Evie said she'd, "gone back up north." This was stunning news. She was supposed to return to Tougaloo and finish college. Her entire family had gone, too, Evie said. That's why the house was empty.

"She done gone back to Elkhart," Giles added, as if he'd suddenly faded into the conversation.

I probed further but they knew nothing more, just that the decision was sudden.

"I'm sure Sharon went to the funeral," I said.

Seeming more alert, Giles said, "That's right. Lef' right after."

Evie nodded.

"Did she leave an address, phone number, anyway I could contact her?" I said.

For the first time, Giles turned his head slowly and cut his eyes sharply on me. "Didn't leave none," he said in a short strong voice. "She gone!"

There are moments when a person knows its time to move on and this was one of those moments. I told them I enjoyed my visit, that it was good to see both of them again, then I bid farewell. As I was descending the porch steps, I glanced back and told them if ever they spoke with Sharon Rose again to give her my regards, and they nodded.

"Come to see us again, Sammy" Evie said.

"I just might do that," I said, turned and gave a final wave.

*   *   *

I drove to Atlanta thinking of nothing but Sharon's sudden and puzzling change of plans. She was too responsible just to up and leave school, her future and her work with the Movement. What could possibly have happened? For a long time, acknowledging her existence and having to carry on as though nothing happened was like scratching the worst itch of my life.

Eventually, over time, it went away.

PART III
Forty Years Later

24

All of us, I guess, have our own way of looking behind us. I do it at night when I'm in bed, the lights are off and I'm rehearsing the day's events, scanning for any red flags. It is still there, the ineluctable anxiety I've carried with me over the years, the glances over my shoulder that cause the years to evaporate, and I see it all again—the night, the hooded eyes, the gravel road, the bridge, the dark moon-reflected river below. From that point on, my whole life has been spent living beneath a threatening storm. I saw the movie *Deliverance* and shuddered at the last scene, at that lone scaly hand rising from the lake.

To the best of my knowledge, the crime, as with Early's murder which I had followed, remains unsolved. Its files gather dust and mold in some metal filing cabinet, in some dark room of the Holmes County Courthouse. They await the raw ambition of someone who wants his or her fifteen minutes of fame to become Attorney General or Governor, who knows. Anyone who can solve a forty-year-old crime always draws a spotlight.

It was not the perfect crime. There was nothing perfect or intentional about it. Yet, the more distance from the occurrence, paradoxically the more perfect it seemed. Hiding behind a clerical robe, conducting the funeral of the man I killed, I was not even suspected. I managed my way through the sequence of events without even a blink of suspicion. How long could the concealment last? One day at a time, forty years' worth—through seminary, marriage, two daughters, one church appointment after another, up the ecclesiastical ladder I've moved, laying down distance from the crime.

Then two events unmasked that thin counterfeit security and sent jolts straight to my heart. The first I read about in the *Atlanta Constitution*: FORMER KLANSMAN INDICTED IN THE MURDER OF THREE CIVIL RIGHTS WORKERS. The fact his name was Killen was of little consequence. The crime he allegedly committed, its place and time chilled me to the bone.

The other event, just days following the first, was a phone call. The day was Saturday, March 19, 2005. Evie had called. Giles was dying and had asked for me. I'd kept in touch with him over the years by letter and by phone. I knew he was well into his nineties but never thought of his dying. He was one of those characters we all know, the kings and queens of the "Not Yet!" They would live forever.

Her voice breaking, Evie said she wanted me to conduct his funeral. Another minister she did not name would be assisting. I told her I was sorry to hear this news and honored to be asked to help. I'd check my schedule and get back with her. I *was* a bishop, and I did have a busy schedule.

I needed to think about her request. I'd felt so far away from that place, I'd never thought of returning. It was too full of my past, too much to revisit. But I did want to see Giles. I did want to assist in his funeral, whenever that might be. Burying the man responsible for who I was and what I had become was more than an honor; it was a hallowed and sacred rite.

But there was another reason I wanted to return, someone else. The last I'd heard, Sharon Rose had "gone back up north." That was forty years ago. Giles was her paternal uncle. They were close. If she was still alive, she would be there. She, the only witness—by legal definition accessory, accomplice—to my deed. And the consenting adult in our other shared sin of passion that summer. There was love, then, I thought. A love made all the stronger by who we were and could not become. Time and circumstance change feelings, but she still held a special place in my heart.

I had no idea how she felt about me. I had not seen her since that terrible summer night. She just disappeared from my life. Often, I've wondered about her and been afraid to ask, afraid the answer might disturb those seeming quiet waters of distance. I've heard it said that history has no energy. But it has a way of fiercely scratching and clawing its way back into our lives.

I called Evie back and told her I would leave as soon as possible and, yes, I would assist with the funeral which. hopefully, would be years away.

Once on the road, it felt good to be going home.

I had made the drive many times but left Atlanta at six o'clock in the morning to give myself ample time. I was on a relatively new four-lane. In Birmingham, I knew to take the Arkadelphia exit. I followed the overhead signs guiding me into the right lane. My blinker was on. At the last second, as though some inexplicable force took over, I veered back into the mainstream of traffic.

*　*　*

Four hours later, I intersected Interstate 55 at Winona, Mississippi, and turned south. At Mount Pleasant, I exited down a ramp onto the old two-lane state highway and into a cluster of convenience stores and the parking lot of a topless bar. Next to it was a liquor store. Colorful neon beer signs shone in the windows of the quick stops. When I left Holmes County in the summer of '64, the place was dry as the Sahara and you couldn't buy a *Playboy* magazine within fifty miles, maybe a hundred. The city limits sign still said Mount Pleasant; the population was still 201. Apparently, no one was willing to admit the change. I glanced at my watch, a little past ten. Time enough to do what I needed to do and get to New Albany by mid-afternoon.

I drove into town. The same buildings were there, no cars parked along the sidewalk in front of them, no people going in and out. Doors were padlocked, windows broken and boarded up. The place looked like a ghost town. Only in the bank was a light on, and the bank's name was still painted in gold on the windows. The Mount Pleasant Bank and Trust, one of the few banks in the country that didn't fold during the Great Depression. The word Trust seemed larger than the others and justly so.

The church was still there, as churches usually are, the plots they occupy sacred ground. It appeared to have a fresh coat of white paint but nothing else about it looked new. The annex was the same size, no new additions, a reflection of population drain, lost members. I drove on down the street to where the parsonage should have been.

All that remained was a weed-choked, faint brick perimeter outlining the foundation. Nearby, a large oak was split down the middle, its dead limbs twisted as though tortured by some fierce and terrible wind. Or a mighty bolt of lightning. I thought perhaps a tornado had touched down, leaving everything else around intact, for no other lot on that block or the next had that ravaged and devastated look about it, as though this one was singled out for destruction. Some folks might say singled out for judgment.

I got out of the car and walked to the place in the side yard where less grass grew. The Kerosene from the burning cross had left its mark. I picked up a long stick and crossed the threshold of what I estimated to have been the front door. I stood there, in space blanketed by seasons of falling leaves from surrounding trees that were still intact. I poked the stick through the soft mulch and with its tip flipped over a slab of compost, a viscous paste of cinder and ash. The strong smell of charred debris and congealed humus rose and I realized then the house had burned, possibly by the lightning bolt I'd suspected. I eyed the ground where a universe of disturbed insects swirled and scrambled aimlessly toward another dark home.

I moved a few steps and repeated the motion, flipping and pushing aside the thick mantel, tapping on blackened rubble of gray-smoked bits of broken bottles, soot-glazed shards of dishes and bowls, cans and lids and bottle caps almost oxidized to soil. Something hard jarred the stick. I stooped and with a forefinger made a groove in the black loam around the object. I worked it back and forth then, with a sucking sound, pulled the piece from the moist sediment. It was the size of a large apple and heavy as lead. Moving it around in my hands, I tried to guess its identity. There were groves along one side and notches across the top. I looked around and discovered I was standing in what would have been the utility room at the rear of the carport. Mystery solved. I was holding the one means of saving grace with a congregation. I had in my hands what was left of a lawnmower, probably the same I had used decades ago.

I knelt down and laid the little motor back into its cavity of layered years. I continued to look around in that drear square-footage of ruin, not even sure what I was looking for. Perhaps I was looking for that ministry of my youth, the rare innocence of that time when I stood for something and held firm. When I had no fear. All I could be sure of was that this place had once been full of a commitment and vision that was gone, as if it had never existed. With those thoughts, I wondered how I continued in the ministry; how I ever became a bishop.

Looking back on that day, I recall something the writer James Salter said in *Burning The Days*: "Sometimes you are aware when your great moments are happening and sometimes, they arise from the past." Perhaps that's what I was looking for, a great moment.

I got back into the car and continued on, heading west toward Acona. I knew about Post-Traumatic Stress Disorder. I had the symptoms— flashbacks, nightmares, feelings of reoccurrence, avoidance of the place of the trauma. I knew of relaxation treatments for coping with the symptoms, but I also knew there was no cure. A person could go for years after the trauma and any sight, noise, smell, taste or touch pushed a button in the brain and the tape rolled again. One psychological source I read said *in vivo* therapy was effective, revisiting the scenes with a therapist or other emotional support. I had no therapist. The only emotional support available was a Presence. I wasn't sure if this was the therapy I needed, but it seemed right.

I passed the same houses, plus a number of doublewides I was sure had not been there, then I saw the C.M.E. Bethel Church. The small brick structure in white trim, white steeple, looked new. But nothing else had changed. There was the same curve in the road, the same pasture across the way and the same trees surrounded the church, only they were larger.

I parked my car and got out. I climbed the steps and tried the latch on the double front doors. They were open, but I did not go in; I knew the floor plan by heart. I walked around to the back of the church, paced a distance from the back wall to a point now covered with undergrowth—sumac and sassafras and honeysuckle, that unforgettable sweet aroma, the irony.

He stops a moment and sets the can on the ground. He looks around and hikes his robe and whisks something from his hip pocket ... My heart revs up, my breathing quickens. I walk back to the wall ... My hand hits something that moves on the window ledge. A loose brick. I grip it firmly with one hand and begin hurriedly working it ... I slip around the corner of the wall and hurl a brick toward the car ....

I remember the direction of its arc and what I did later with both of the bricks. I walked to the spot and pushed back the brush. I got on my knees and picked at the ground. Gouging deeper, I flipped up small brick chips, the larger, broken pieces I'd scattered in the woods that night, no telling where.

*   *   *

The bridge was harder to find. The location of county roads had not changed, but my memory of them had dimmed. I knew to go to Tchula and take a county road from there to Swifttown north of Belzoni. The road was more pocked and buckled than I remembered with freshly plowed fields either side. A dumpster was in the spot where I'd parked my car that evening. My heart beat faster as I approached the old trestle bridge, surprised it was still in use. No traffic was coming and I stopped in the middle of it, idled the engine and got out. I stood beneath the dark steel trusses and smelled the black creosoted timbers.

"You've got to pull them tighter," she says.

"I'm pulling them tight as I can."

"I don't think this is going to work," she says. "We should've buried him."

The foliage was so thick, I couldn't see the river. But I could hear it's rippling murmur and recalled the loud splash, one I would hear over and over, asleep or awake. I still wondered how the body came loose from the concrete blocks. It had rained several days after we dumped it, and that's what I guessed happened. The river became suddenly swollen and mad with runoff.

*   *   *

I walked across the small silent cemetery. The grounds were freshly mowed, well kept. Unlike that hot August funeral day, a cool breeze blew in from the surrounding trees—oaks, cedars and sycamores, with scattered splashes of white dogwood and pink redbud. I thought of the plot my wife and I had chosen in Atlanta, of the heavy daily noise and traffic that would jar our vaults. I walked past toppled plastic vases stuffed with Styrofoam and plastic flowers, past a few sprays of yellow daffodils until I stood beside the grave, now matted with Saint Augustine, and faced the tombstone that said Top Hunsucker, it's shadow leaning slightly at a one o'clock angle. I felt I was looking at a still life of my sin.

I stood a moment looking at the name, recalling images of the big man, images I wanted to remember—his presence at Sunday church, potluck suppers and dinners-on-the-ground. I knelt and said a prayer, the Holy Communion prayer of confession. I had said it a thousand times perfunctorily and knew it by heart. This time, it would shake me to my core. "Merciful God, I confess that I have not loved you with my whole heart. I have failed to be an obedient servant. I have not done your will, I have broken your law, I have rebelled against your love, I have not loved my neighbor …."

After the "Amen!" I stood and walked away. Like the end of that funeral, one anxiety ended, and another began. I knew my pilgrimage did not cleanse me. More was needed. Easter was just days ahead of me. I thought about that, how all of our resurrections are ahead of us.

New Albany was almost three hours away. But I had one more stop to make, a visit that might take longer. A lot longer.

* * *

The building was small and square and made of concrete blocks. Originally, it had been painted a light gray color, ostensibly to reflect cheerful modernity, bring life to the block where older county buildings cast a drab municipal glum. Now, it was a dirty weathered color, not even gray, but darker, splotched with mildew grunge and ground sweat. It had cross-barred windows and a cross-barred door. The large black letters stencil-painted over the door said HOLMES COUNTY SHERIFF'S DEPARTMENT.

For a long time, I sat parked outside mulling over the case that apparently, like Early's, had never been solved. A lot of people die, and no one knows what happened to them. They just fade from sight without ever being missed. But people knew about Top Hunsucker; his death had been in the news. I thought of all the sleepless nights since he died at my hands and wondered if my anguish was self-pity and self-contempt or something else, perhaps an obsession with purity. Or a combination of all. I reasoned Hunsucker's death was in defense of another. But it still gnawed at me. That and the fact I apparently got away with it. Apparently.

I finally got out of the car, opened a heavy steel door and stepped inside.

The interior was simple. Just inside the door was a small room with a glass window, like those used in ticket boxes at cinemas. Through the window, I saw radio equipment and a deputy in khaki shirt and pants sitting in a swivel chair. He was smoking a cigar and seemed to be pondering a rack of padlocked rifles on the wall in front of him. There was a larger room which was probably the Sheriff's Office. Down a short hallway through another steel door were the cells.

The deputy grunted as he pushed himself up, as though it took great effort, and walked to the window. He was a young, stockily built black man. I identified myself and quickly, before I lost courage, told him I had information on the death of Top Hunsucker, a murder which took place forty-one years ago. The deputy's face screwed up in a puzzled look and he scratched his head.

"Don't recall any Hunsucker. Forty years is a long time. We don't have records back that far, not here in this building, anyway."

"It would have been the summer of '64."

"My, my. I wasn't even born then."

"No, I guess you weren't," I mumbled under my breath. He was an underling and probably wouldn't know anyway, even if he *had* been born then.

As I stood there looking around that small county jail, taking in all its simple rural trappings of law and order, the events of that summer flooded my thoughts. I looked back at the deputy and told him I guessed I'd made a mistake and was in the wrong county.

"What'd you say your name was?" he said as I was leaving.

"I didn't," I said and closed that heavy door behind me.

* * *

The afternoon was waning, the sun's soft light filling the sky as I crossed the last river bottom and saw the water tower with the big letters NEW ALBANY on it. The streets of the town had not changed, only my memory of their configuration. Giles' house was in a part of town called the Dum. I asked my mother once why it was called the Dum. She said the town was first settled by the French, and she'd read that the word "Dum" came from a Latin phrase that meant, "While I breathe, I hope." Reflecting on my first visit to the Dum, almost half a century ago, the phrase resonated.

* * *

"Where're we going next?" I said to Giles as we finished dropping off a load of slab wood.

"My house," he said.

I asked why we were going there and not back to the sawmill for another load of wood. It was early afternoon. He said he'd picked up a medicine prescription for his wife and had to take it to her along with one more he picked up for another lady. I asked why the drugstore couldn't deliver it like they did to our house.

He leaned, spit over the side of the wagon, then turned intense sad eyes on me. "Just don't."

We rode on, trusty ole Bud leading the way, clip-clopping along the narrow, thinly paved streets, swinging his head left and right, turning here and there, without guidance from his driver. This was his world, one he could travel blind. He might be for all I knew. I recalled something Giles had said about mules, that as beleaguered and maligned as they were, there wouldn't be a South without them. They were smart if you cared for them and treated them kindly and stubborn only when mistreated. Most folks mistreated them because they thought they were ignorant and dumb. "No living thing wants to go through life being mistreated, and being stubborn to mistreatment is just being smart," he said. That's why white folks in the South compared them to colored folk, thinking both to be dumb when, in fact, both were surviving the only way they knew how, by being stubborn. The look in Giles' eyes that day when he uttered those words conveyed a broader and deeper knowledge of history.

Deep into the Dum riding with Giles I went. Farther, I thought, than any white person had ever gone. Further ever than any explorer into the heart of Africa. I saw people and sights I'd never seen before and people I wanted to see and didn't. Not a single white person. I was the only one.

Giles seemed to notice my growing discomfort and did something he'd never done before. I didn't think about it at the time, as long as we'd been together why he hadn't. Looking back brings the understanding I could not have had then. Giles was safe, in his own place, among his own people. Without fear for me or himself, he wrapped his big arm around me and pulled me close. I smelled him when he did, felt his sweat. He held me close a few moments, my head pressed against his thick shoulder. He said nothing, but I heard all I needed to hear in that silence as I relaxed and took in that strange, new world.

Women and pigtailed children sat in open doors, some with colorful bandannas and rags wrapped around their heads. They just sat, looking out over the cluttered dirt yards, beyond the streets with no sidewalks and no curbs, as though they were watching something far away that was not coming their way. There were no men at the houses. They were all clustered around the small stores tucked in here and there among the houses, with only a soda drink or snuff sign hanging on an eave or over a door to tell you it was a store.

Amidst all that was broken down and torn down and falling down, the flowers stood out. They were everywhere; bordering the small yards and rotting porches, running along the weather-scuffed house-sidings and along the tattered and broken fencerows. It seemed there were thousands of them, blossoming from that litter and scrubbage, blooming in contradiction to the ruin and deterioration—roses, zinnias, crepe myrtle, chrysanthemums, hydrangeas and salvia. Our black gardener, David Wade, whose life my father had saved, taught me all the names. *While I breathe, I hope.* The flowers said it all

* * *

Entering the Dum once more, fifty years later, Ole Bud helped me. Once I turned off Main Street, I remembered after three blocks the trusty mule turned left, then right after one block and left again, and there it was, the long hill leading up to Giles' house.

The house had been painted a light blue. The wisteria vine had taken over the porch, and the large gum tree still stood in front. Behind the house, I could see the wagon, that ark of my youth. It was leaning against a small shed that tilted precariously with it, as though both had aged together and would fall together. Bud was surely dead by now. The scene looked like an old painting hanging on the sky, the sun descending behind it.

Several cars were parked along the front of the house and in the drive. I parked behind a red pickup down the hill. No one had seen me. I did not immediately get out. I heard a train whistle in the distance. It was a sound that had not changed over time, but one I heard differently then. In my childhood when I heard the whistle, I was usually tucked into bed at night and on the brink of sleep. It was a happy soothing sound, one coming toward me filled with promise. Now, the sound is a symbol of sadness, the resonance of something leaving.

I thought about what was between me and the house and who, besides Giles and Evie, might be inside. Forty years, forty-one to be exact, was a long time. Sharon and I were about the same age. She wanted to be called Shar in those days, but I will always remember her as Sharon, Sharon Rose. The rose of Sharon.

I had changed some. The shrinkage of cartilage may have dropped me an inch. My hair was a salt-and-pepper gray. My wife still told me I was handsome as ever. I wondered what the years had done to Sharon Rose. I imagined she, too, had turned gray and was possibly shorter, maybe even plump like some older women are prone to become as they age. One thing will not have changed. Regardless of the effects of time, I expected the beauty. In that long ago summer, in every way, she was that.

I remained in the car a while longer to gather my thoughts, think about what I'd say and let the memories, stirred by the long drive and anticipation, settle.

But they were just starting up.

25

I opened the door and got out. As I began walking up the hill toward the house, a voice called out, "He's here, Evie," the absence of my name an indication I was expected. Never one to calculate ages well, I worked the math and guessed Evie and Giles were both in their nineties. She came through the screen door and wobbled cautiously down the steps to greet me. She wore a white turban and a bright calico dress. An old beauty shone through wrinkles and sagging flesh that was not fat, but aged muscle and sinew. Once she had been tall and stout. Now, she was stooped and moved with a shuffling gait. Her voice was strong and firm as she held to my hand and led me up the steps, her grip as firm as it was the first day I met her.

"He wanted to see you, Sammy. He's been talking 'bout nothing but you. Now, he don't look too good, I'll tell you that."

"He'll look good to me," I said as I held her hand and followed her through the crowd of strangers on the porch, through the screen door and into a dimly lit living room. Though I'd only been inside the house once briefly, the day Giles took me, it looked the same. The old rocker was still there, in the same place. An electric refrigerator had replaced the ice box. Comic papers still covered the walls, and the picture of Jesus still hung crooked on the wall above the couch.

Then I saw a cluster of faces, one in particular among the others, a vague resemblance, its light tan standing out. She was tall with silver gray hair pulled back into a chignon and wore a white blouse and black skirt, black heels that anchored her securely where she stood, her arms crossed. She was leaning against a wall. We were about the same age, but the person I saw looked much younger. Her figure and lines, the full face, her total look was that of a woman in touch with who she was. That was the confidence I saw, the serene dignity I remembered.

She approached me and spoke first.

"Sam Ransom." Her hand was extended but I couldn't shake it.

We hugged.

"Sharon," I whispered, holding her awkwardly at the shoulders, a shudder traveling my body. I felt her, too, trembling in the embrace. "My God, you look great."

"You look good yourself. How long has it been?" she said taking an arm's length look, still gripping my shoulders.

I sensed others observing this reunion and wanted to find a place where we could talk, but Giles was the reason I came and Evie, her outstretched hand hinting, was waiting. "Too long," I said, responding to her question.

"You go ahead," Sharon said and released her hands from my shoulders. "Uncle Giles is more important right now. We can visit later."

Evie led me into a smaller room. Low, afternoon sunlight shined starkly through a curtainless window. Through the warped panes of the window, I saw again the old wagon, its tongue angled on the ground and pointing toward the window, toward me.

The glare of light softened as people and objects materialized from the shadows. At first, I didn't recognize the person on the metal frame bed. He was lying on his back, motionless. His head lay flat on shapeless pillows. A soiled, stringy rag covered his forehead. Layers of frayed and faded quilts were pulled up under his chin so that only his head and outstretched arms were visible. Aging had shortened him. His full face of bulbous cheeks had wasted to thin ridges of bone that glistened in the light. His eyes were cloudy and gray, his gaze rigid and fixed. The air was palpable with death.

On a small table by the bed were a washbasin, a bottle of medicine and a glass with a teaspoon in it. Two middle-aged women I did not know sat in chairs on the other side of the bed. I saw Lula standing in a corner, her hands prayerfully folded beneath her chin. When our eyes met, it was almost too much. She came around the bed and embraced me. When my mother died years ago, Lula was the first in that hospital room to hold me. She said no words then and said none now. Her arms around me spoke. After a lengthy hug, she released me and returned quietly to her place in the corner.

At the end of the bed stood a tall man, much younger than the others in the room. His head was bowed, his silent lips moving in prayer. He wore a black suit and black tie and had a pastoral look about him. Evie had told me another would be helping with the funeral.

Evie leaned over and whispered into Giles' ear. He strained his head slightly and turned to look. His thin smile lay in a net of wrinkles. He blinked slowly. I saw that same dreamy gaze of a sun-shot summer afternoon when he described judgment day, as though he was seeing it happen before his very eyes and the aged vehicle on which he rode his personal chariot to salvation.

Upward, slowly, came a hand. I reached out and held it, felt what was left of the strength that had pulled me time and again into the wagon, a strength that swung a belt at bullies one Saturday at Gravlee's. The touch of his hand plugged me into that glorious time, memories I thought would die if I let go. So I stood there holding his hand, our eyes connected, memories running like a river.

He pushed himself up and, in a raspy whisper, said, "Sammy ..."

I sensed his struggle and wanted to help. "Yessir, Uncle Giles. I can hear you."

"Gettin' ready to change wagons ... ready ... to ...." He stopped and caught his breath. His chest was heaving, as though he'd been saving his energy for this single moment.

"Yessir, yessir, that's right," the suited man at the end of the bed chanted.

The women moaned. Lula sighed.

Evie laid a hand on my shoulder.

I fought back tears.

"Just changin' wagons ... that's all. Yessir, yessir," gumming his lips, talking to himself the way old people do. "It's been a long time." His neck looked tortured the way it was turned, and he wrenched it further. "What you up to these days?"

With quick strokes—squeezing everything into the precious seconds I felt remained—I winnowed my life to a handful of sentences. I told him about my wife, my two children: one, a son, a minister; the other a daughter, a missionary; both married and with their own families. He'd known about seminary. I'd told him that long ago, forty years. But I told him again adding the various churches I'd served in Mississippi, Florida and Georgia, my teaching stint at Emory in Atlanta, where I lived now, all of the bio rushed as though my life had been a rocket taking off. Then, I told him I was a bishop.

"Who he?" he said.

I explained.

His eyes flared and his mouth stretched into a wide toothless smile. "Sounds kinda high and mighty," he said, still smiling, breathing unevenly.

"Guess it does at that."

"Never seen you high and mighty."

"Never seen myself as high and mighty. I need to be brought low," I said, my voice filled with emotion, almost cracking.

I felt his unblinking eyes piercing my soul.

"All us do," he murmured.

I looked around at the others in the room, making eye contact with each then back at him. "But not for the reasons I do."

He was listening, his eyes still on me, something in them telling me he sensed an urgency. In that brief time, the sun had moved a little down the sky, enough in its late descent that it flashed an orange slash across the bed. Giles grimaced at the brightness as though in pain. The man standing at the foot of the bed noticed, too, and moved to block the glare. As he stepped into the sudden surge of light, I saw, for the first time, his color was not theirs … but mine. We were in the twenty-first century. Race relations had come a long way, black ministers serving white churches and vice-versa. But I wondered who he was, this white man in the depths of the Dum, ministering in the heart of the black community. He had that clerical aplomb and adroitness, that measured pastoral cadence of their race in his whispered prayers.

Giles was still holding my hand, then he let go, waved limply at the others then toward the door, a clear gesture of dismissal for them to leave.

Slowly, they departed, the tall sophisticated white man closing the door behind them.

"Now," he said with a single nod of his head, his eyes looking into mine as if to say, "*I understand, I'm listening.*"

"Thank you, Uncle Giles," I said. "I needed to speak with you alone."

He turned his body. "Bump up this here pillow, Sammy, so's I can see you better."

I reached over and pushed the pillow higher.

"Good," he said. "Glad you come."

"I wanted to come."

"You see Sharon Rose?" he nodded toward the door. "She out there."

"Yessir. She looks good."

"Always look good. Y'all had some good times."

"We did. That's something I need to talk about."

The gummy smile evaporated and his face turned serious. "Sho'nuff. You been totin' it a long time."

I didn't know what to say, his glaucous eyes suddenly lasers stripping me, but they were not condemning. "How did you know?" I finally managed.

"Sharon, she come in, 'bout nervous as you, said she needed to be free of somethin'."

"She told you everything."

"Everything's a lot. Doubt she told me everything." He stopped to get his breath, opened his mouth to speak, then looked at the door. "Ner'mind. She can tell you."

"Tell me what?"

"She can tell you."

"But what happened between us is not everything," I said.

He grinned and said, "I ain't here long enough for everything."

"You remember once my asking you if you had ever killed a man?"

"Sho do. Killed more'n one."

"I killed a man."

I was waiting for the out-of-sync blink again but he just stared at me, his eyes glistening with moisture. At first he said nothing, just nodded. Then, "You saved Sharon Rose."

"She told you."

He nodded again and I saw, shaken with the nod, tears roll down his cheeks onto the quilts around his neck. "Early." That was all he whispered, then repeated. "Early."

I cannot put into words my emotions of that moment. I was trying to put together what Giles knew and didn't know. He knew Early and Sharon were close; then something happened. I figured he knew now the "something."

"Early died for us, for me and Sharon," I said.

He opened his mouth but couldn't speak.

"I killed the man who killed him. I conducted his funeral. I fornicated with my friend's girlfriend. I'm a bishop. I've lived a lie. I need to live the truth. I need to be forgiven."

He reached over and grabbed my hand. "Sammy, cain't undo what the Lawd's done done. He fo'gave me long time ago. He fo'gave you long time ago, so long ago He don't remember Hisself."

"I know. But I need to be forgiven by flesh and bone. I need to feel it."

His eyes narrowed as though angry. "And you the bishop talkin' this nonsense. You and Sharon Rose, she say 'bout the same. 'Cept she ain't no bishop. I wonna crawl outta this bed and whop you both." The pseudo-anger in his eyes disappeared and he flashed that toothless grin again. He squeezed my hand, raised up and lifted his other arm into the air to embrace me but fell back onto the bed, his head collapsing onto the pillow. I leaned over and kissed his forehead. A limp hand went again into the air, and he looked at the door and motioned. I felt him going. I opened the door and called the others in.

Lula entered first, followed by the two women and the young man, all resuming their places in the small room. Giles raised his head and looked around.

"Sharon Rose," he said in a weak whisper.

Evie stuck her head out the door and motioned. Sharon entered and stood behind Evie. Giles strained his neck again and looked at Sharon. He made a circular motion with his hand, then it fell limply on the quilts. He wanted her to come around the bed to the other side.

I couldn't see her. She was behind me. I sensed a hesitation, heard the heeled footsteps and watched her move around the bed and stand opposite me. But her eyes were not on Giles; nor were mine. They were locked on each other's.

I shall never forget that look as long as I live. If I saw what she saw in mine, she saw a yearning to another time, one not forgotten and still much alive in our shared memories—riding in the ark of our youth, its captain high on the seat shaking ole Bud's reins. She saw the sadness of a lost friend, who rode with us in those golden days and should be standing there with us. She saw the shared guilt. She saw the pain.

Her lips quivered, a faint tremulous smile. I looked down at Giles' wide, toothless grin. He raised both arms, an obvious gesture for us to hold his hands. Sharon reached for one, I the other. We stood there holding his hands. Still smiling, he squeezed, and we squeezed back. I thought of the word atonement, how it broke down: at-one-ment. We were one, Sharon and I ... and Giles. And I felt at one with myself.

Moments passed. Sharon and I still held Giles' hands. I knew that feel, had sensed it hundreds of times before, of the air in a room beginning to turn to death. I looked at Lula, but she'd covered her eyes with her hands. Hundreds of times I'd stood by the dying in hospitals, homes, roadsides. I did not always know exactly what to say but was able to say something comforting. In that moment, no words came to mind. My mentor, the man who shaped me and was responsible for my ministry, was dying. I'd just received from him the forgiveness I'd sought and needed. And now I, the bishop, could say nothing. I thought if the right feeling came, the words would come. The right feeling was there, and still the words did not come. I looked at Sharon. We leaned over and kissed him on his cheeks. I said, "I love you, Uncle Giles." She whispered something I couldn't hear, but whatever it was our words made him smile again.

Sharon raised her head and glanced at the young man at the foot of the bed. He began moving his hands and murmuring what I thought were probably the prayers of last rites. The words came slowly, meditatively. I caught a few phrases and recognized them. They were from the *United Methodist Book of Discipline*.

Giles struggled, pulled on our hands as if he wanted to sit up, then lay back. His lips moved to speak, but nothing came out of that trembling mouth. Then, in a final effort, came one word, "bliss," the final sound escaping his lips like a hiss, expiring, fading, and his eyes closed. His long, boney fingers loosed in our hands and went limp onto the bed. A cloud passed over the setting sun and the room darkened, but he was illumined by a seraphic glow. I had the clear feeling that all of my life had led to this moment, and all that followed would lead to no place of any significance.

26

"Tell me about *you*," I said, taking the initiative.

In the dusk light, we were leaning against the wagon. She'd suggested we get some fresh air and once outside we were drawn in that direction.

"You first, Sam Ransom," Sharon said, a resoluteness I recalled beneath the smile.

She listened intently as I recapped the history I'd told Giles, though with more detail. When I told her about my wife and children, she smiled approvingly. I told her that last year I'd been elected a bishop at the jurisdictional conference.

She smiled. "I know," she said.

"You know?"

"The young man in Giles room is my son," she said, the proud smile widening. "His name is Rand. He's a minister in the United Methodist Church, a pastor of a church in Fort Wayne, Indiana. He was a delegate at a different jurisdictional conference but knew of the bishops elected in the Southeastern Conference. He was reading off the names of those elected and I heard your name."

"My, my," was all I could say.

She went on to tell me he had a wife and three children. They lived up north near her, where she'd found a home, not in Elkhart but Mishawaka, near South Bend.

She then spoke of herself. She'd finished college, got her RN degree at a small school I'd never heard of. She'd worked at a number of different hospitals. She lived a quiet life, spent time with her grandkids who came often, or she went to them.

"So, you're retired now," I said.

"Absolutely not," she said with mock indignation. "I'm working at a nursing home. Retirement is a sin," she continued. "I never married."

"You mean … ?" I said.

"He doesn't know."

This was what Giles had said she'd tell me. There was a long pause, a silence I couldn't fill. The words were not there. As fond as I am of saying the spirit moves where it will, nothing moved then. Absolutely nothing.

She spoke again. "When he was in first grade, he wondered why he didn't have a daddy like all the other children. It was around Christmas. There was a school play. He was in it and wondered why there was not a daddy watching him too."

"What did you tell him?"

"I told him he had a daddy, just that his daddy was a long way away and couldn't be there. That was all his mind could handle at that time."

"And later?"

"We were on a picnic. He raised the question again about his father. He was eleven. He was very intelligent, so I had to be just as intelligent. I told him about the summer of '64. By that time, he'd read about it in school and seen programs on television. I simply told him that things happened that might not otherwise have happened. I gave no excuses. I did not tell him I loved the person, just that he was someone very special. I knew to give no details. To do so would have opened Pandora's box. He's very inquisitive, but he never asked again."

"Why did you not tell me back then? Surely, you knew?"

"Yes, I knew or was pretty sure I knew. You remember that time, all the confusion. We were collaborators, co-conspirators. I just wanted to protect my baby."

Then it hit me. "In other words, the long arm of the law."

"Yes. If anyone found out, I could go to prison, which meant my child would either grow up in prison or in a foster home. That thought nearly broke me. I knew only one thing to do." She drew a hand across an eye, as though to smother a tear. "The authorities told me not to leave the county, but they didn't tell me not to leave the state. I had relatives up north who would take me in, where I'd never be found. From there, you know the rest, at least the big picture. I didn't want to burden you with that truth, in case you were asked. There are no interesting details. There was not then, nor has there been since, anyone else."

"There could have been," I said. "You were, still are, beautiful in every way."

She cupped a sheepish hand against her forehead then removed it, her eyes looking directly at mine. "Sam Ransom. You haven't changed," she said through a half-smirk, half-smile.

Leaning there against the old wagon, the aroma of its cypress walls still detectable, an old energy was working once again. I could feel it and I knew she did, too. There was nothing we could do about it or would. But in those few moments, we enjoyed the feeling all over again, as though transported back in time to those eternal moments, to that wild summer of real love, real intimacy, real nights and real days, and ephemeral dreams. Just the two of us in the corner of that burned-out sanctuary, completely and totally unaware of the future we were creating.

I wanted to reach out and touch her. Her eyes said she wanted to do the same but we were in sight of others. We had reconnected and that seemed the important thing. We knew when the funeral was over, we might never see each other again, that cold prospect intermingling with the warmth of reunion. And our departure was not far away. The sun had set and we had little light left. But there was one thing we hadn't talked about.

"Before we have to go," she said, "whatever happened about that man?"

"You mean Hunsucker?"

She looked toward the house, an insurance glance. No one was near. "Yes, I didn't remember his name."

"Every day I think of him," I said. "Every day."

"I don't think of him every day, but I've thought about him," she said. "There's a time to kill and a time to heal. The Bible says that. I'm a pacifist. Martin Luther King was my hero. But there is a time to act, especially in defense of the life of another. Timing can do that, cut across our beliefs. You saved my life."

Reluctantly, I nodded. One way or another, Sharon Rose Word would have survived. She was wired for survival—supple, tough, righteous. Her face-off against Hunsucker I will never forget: *I don't have any car keys. That's not my car. And don't call me nigger again.* And he didn't. "I had to conduct his funeral," I said. "That's why I wasn't at Early's. The services were at the same time, on the same day."

"So, that's why you weren't there. I thought you just didn't want to face *me* again, that seeing me would be too painful. That almost kept me from going."

"But you went."

"Yes."

"And you kept on going."

She didn't respond.

"I drove up later, went by your house after I went by the cemetery. Everyone was gone. Giles said back to Elkhart. I nearly crumbled."

"I told you why."

"Yes, but I had no inkling then."

A shout from the front porch: "Mother, it's getting late. They're putting out the food."

He'd taken off his coat and stood in his shirtsleeves rolled to his elbows. He definitely looked more my color, but he was taller than I.

"Rand, come here, there's someone I want you to meet."

I knocked a hand against hers, gently, a gesture intended to reverse the summons.

"It's all right," she whispered.

As he stepped from the porch and walked toward us, I was looking for those genetic clues of parentage. The casual loose-legged gait was mine, the one my grandfather said looked like a man pushing a plow. There, too, from his neck up, was the facial structure of a Scotch-Irish line. He'd let his hair grow in waves across the front. His carriage was erect, as distinguished as the voice I'd heard earlier. Had I known absolutely nothing else I would have said here is a man of distinction.

I was moved.

We shook hands. His grip was firm, full of confidence. Our eyes met and held a moment, then I looked away, at her. She was smiling. No, beaming.

He and I shared occupational pleasantries. The United Methodist Church is a connectional system. News and names travel rapidly. His membership was in a different jurisdiction, but, as his mother had related, he'd heard of me.

"I believe congratulations are in order, Bishop Ransom," he said, no mention he'd read a list of names to his mother after the election.

Her brows rose and her eyes widened when he said it. She stood with her arms folded looking at us. I sensed the silent pride and something else I could not name. If they are to maintain their mystical, magical quality, there are some moments that should remain, always, undefined.

There are also those moments when it's time to say goodbye. I thought of asking if she needed my help but snuffed the thought as soon as it flared.

I shook his hand, hugged her, kissed her lightly on the cheek and walked away.

I stepped back into the house to say goodbye to Evie. I wanted to speak again with Lula.

Lula was in the living room. She rose from the sofa when I entered and smothered me again with a long hug. She was in her nineties, but her mind did not reflect her age. She began with, "I remember when ..." and never let up. For anyone willing to listen, she told my childhood story, with particular emphasis on those times she took care of me, and included Early in her comments. She finally wound down and sighed, "Lord, it's good to have you home. This is where you belong."

Yes, I told Evie, who was standing and waiting. I would return in a week to assist with the funeral.

I walked onto the porch. Sharon and Rand were still standing by the wagon. I looked back and waved to them. Arm in arm and smiling, they waved back. I wondered about the conversation between them. I wondered why she named him Rand and hoped I knew the answer. As I began walking down the hill, I turned and glanced back at her.

She saw me, smiled thinly, briefly, and waved again.

27

A week later I returned for Giles' funeral. The date was March 27th. Fittingly, it was Easter Sunday.

His home was only a few blocks from the church and the cemetery was behind the church. Sharon's idea added an appropriate touch. The harness and reins were in the shed, stiff and cracked, dust-laden but intact and functional. Lula found someone with a mule on the edge of town near the river and, per her directions, the owners brought it to us. Sharon and I rode up front on the seat. The wagon's rear panel was removed and we'd decided some of Giles' grandchildren could sit on the back as we'd once done, legs swinging. Once more, I held the reins. It wasn't ole Bud pulling us and Giles and Early were missing, but it seemed that time had turned around, the world repeating itself and I was back at the beginning, feeling an old power.

I wondered who was pulling whom as I thought about the person in the casket in the wagon bed behind me, the one person who seemed to draw all the disparate elements of my past together. I thought about the casket and the black pall over it and recalled that cold wet winter day, Giles in his black-hooded rain slicker and the black tarpaulin covering his load and my mother's comment: *Oh my, he'll catch his death.* Death finally did *catch* him. But down the final stretch, Giles gave the reaper a run for his money. After Evie told me his medical history, I decided Giles was truly the king of "Not Yet!" As the pallbearers lifted the casket from its conveyance,

I thought of Giles' earlier words before he died. He was indeed changing wagons, his personal chariot was comin' for to carry him home.

Pilgrim Rest C.M.E. Church was a small, post-office red brick building with two square towers, one shorter than the other. Rand Word and I conducted the service. Only two people there knew it was a father/son team. Sharon sat on the second row with family, behind tuxedoed and white-gloved ushers. I was too overwhelmed to feel anything natural.

In the harsh daylight at the graveside, I could see Early's tombstone two plots away. I recalled the day I bought it. The man at the monument works asked me if I wanted granite or marble. Marble was more expensive, but that was not the reason I chose granite. What color? I'd never thought about the color of a tombstone. I considered black, polished with gold lettering, except the polished effect wouldn't be Early. So I chose the unpretentious black rough granite. On it was his name, Early Holly, dates of birth and death.

I thought about the irony of his name. He was born too early; he died too early. Then this epilogue: *Greater love has no man than this, that he lay down his life for his friends.* The stone was larger than I had planned but the inscription had to fit the monument, the salesman told me. It was appropriate. Early was bigger than life. I later established a scholarship in his honor at Rust College so others could rise above unfortunate circumstances.

After Rand said the committal, I knew it was all over. The goodbyes would move quickly. Sharon and Rand would return to Indiana and I'd make the long drive back to Atlanta. We'd probably never see each other again, but I knew I'd keep up with Rand. We had a legitimate connection in a connectional ministry. Our discussions when we were together had all been perfunctory—about the funeral, protocol and logistics. But I knew, with pride, I would follow his career as long as I lived.

When I pulled out of the cemetery onto the highway, I did not turn east toward Atlanta. I made a final drive through the town to touch some familiar bases, for I knew I would never return.

I drove down Cleveland Street and stopped in front of my former home. After my mother's death, I sold it to a young black couple. The place looked neat and well-kept, better than I'd left it. The azaleas and jonquils my mother had planted were in bloom. On the curb where I was sitting the day

I saw Giles coming down the street, where Early and I sold lemonade, the city had painted the house number. I was tempted to knock on the door and pay a brief visit but decided against it. I had a long drive ahead of me.

I circled my old block, that playground of my youth. The street names—Jackson, Garfield, Peterson—had not changed. On Peterson, I stopped in front of Early's old home and his mother's beauty shop. His mother had died not long after his death. The place was empty, rundown, the small front porch overgrown in—what would I expect— honeysuckle vines. I almost didn't recognize the mimosa tree, its wide branches fanning over the roof. The basketball hoop was still in place, hanging limply from the same tree. The ditch where we played was there along with the shed on the Phyfer place. I sat and thought a moment. Was it possible? I put the car in park, turned off the engine and got out.

I could go to a nearby house and borrow a shovel. There might be one in the old utility shed, but that was unlikely. It was dilapidated and leaning. I removed my suit coat, rolled up my sleeves and opened the trunk. I retrieved a tire wrench. With the sharp end, I could loosen the soil and dig, scoop the dirt out with my hands.

I walked to the rear of the shed. It sat on concrete blocks and I remembered we had picked a spot beneath a rear corner. The area around it was matted with weeds, nutgrass and goldenrod which had to be cleared. I got on my knees and tested the ground with the tool. It was hard. The procedure was going to take longer than I thought. I began chipping away the topsoil. I needed to be careful. This was a fragile keepsake, if it was still there. Beyond the thick layer of red clay the soil began to soften. Gently and carefully, using the wrench as a probe, I was able to penetrate deeper, removing loose soil with my hands as I went. A few more prods and I heard a light *clank*.

After trenching around the area and working the soil back and forth, I carefully grasped the Mason jar and pulled it from the ground. The lid was rusticated and brittle. I wiped the dirt away and held it up in the sunlight. There inside, as I had imagined it might look, curled up like a chrysalis, was the note.

Fifty years of time, moisture and grit had sealed the top. After tapping lightly with the tire tool and several tries, it twisted open. It was my note in my handwriting. Still, I felt I was violating some sacred chamber.

With two trembling fingers, I pulled out the small scrap of paper, smoothed it in the gritty palm of my hand and read, in the crude penciled scrawling of a twelve-year-old:

Sunday July 4, 1954
Early and Sammy
Blood Brothers

It was important to me at the time to put his name first. Below "Blood Brothers," I had to look closely to see them, two faded blotches, the stains where we touched the paper after making razor slices on our thumbs and pressing them together. In those days of innocence, to us we were blood brothers. But I knew I could never really *be* his blood brother.

Maybe you don't have the courage 'cause it ain't your cause ... it wadn't your people ....

He was right. I could never know his struggle. No matter how much sympathy I had for the black people in my life, I could never know the road they traveled, the plight they endured. I thought it fitting that he and Giles were buried behind a church called Pilgrim's Rest.

The paper trembling in my hand, I stood there awhile, my eyes fixed upon it, before returning it to the jar. I secured the lid, glanced around to see if anyone was looking. I filled in the gouged hole I'd created and, jar in hand, walked to the car. I would put it in a special place where I would see it every day. More than a remembrance. A memorial. A testimony.

I recall a book I read recently about the summer of '64. It was titled *The Summer That Didn't End.*

And it hasn't.

ACKNOWLEDGEMENTS

Torched: Summer of '64 involved over forty years of writing and research. I began working on it when I was a chaplain above the Arctic Circle on the DEWLine (Distant Early Warning Line) in 1972-1973. The title was *The Pillared Dark*, a phrase taken from Robert Frost's poem, "Come In."

Far in the pillared dark
Thrush music went—
Almost like a call to come in
To the dark and lament.

I wrote several chapters, filed them away, became involved in writing a dissertation and articles for professional psychological and religion journals. In 1990, a person came into my life, a former English teacher. She read the "lost" chapters, thought they had merit. I was inspired to renew the effort and, also, to marry her.

I completed a manuscript, which had gone through several title changes, but was unsure what to do with the final product: *Comin' For To Carry Me Home.* A retired English teacher in Tupelo, Mississippi, Francis Patterson, read the work and said I needed to see Evans Harrington.

"Who is Evans Harrington?" I asked.

"Professor Emeritus of English at Ole Miss."

An appointment was arranged. I met Dr. Harrington, who would become my mentor. At Square Books in Oxford, we sat on the balcony (which is no longer there) overlooking the courthouse square. I delivered the manuscript to him. Several weeks later, we met back, same place, same porch, same table. He delivered the news to me gently: "Joe Edd, there is some good writing here, but I believe this is the novel you had to write to learn how to write a novel."

I was disheartened, but not discouraged and went back to the drawing board. Another manuscript, different title, *Carry Me Home*, was delivered to him at the same place. Evans took the revised manuscript. When we met again, he said I was not there yet with *Carry Me Home* and encouraged me to try something else.

To encapsulate, in 2002, *Land Where My Fathers Died*, was published. Other novels were written that remain unpublished. In that time period, Evans Harrington died in 1997 and I was on my own. Some non-fictional theological works were published and in 2015 a novel, *The Last Page*, was published. In 2016, I began work on *The Prison*, a sequel to *Land Where My Fathers Died*. It was published in winter of 2019.

Amid a flurry of writing and book events, I returned to *Carry Me Home* and more title changes—*Return to Freedom Summer, Greater Love*. Eventually, at long last, I finished *Torched: Summer of '64*.

Besides the gentle guiding hand of Evans Harrington, others were helpful along the way. Over the years, I may have forgotten some of those involved, but the following are documented readers and critics: Dr. John Bryson, my dentist and literary aficionado; author Peggy Webb (arguably the most prolific author in Mississippi history); the late columnist Phyllis Harper, who read each of the later drafts in their evolution; Drs. Gerald and Julie Walton, friends of the Harringtons and steady reviewers over the years (They've read everything I have written); Dr. Roy Ryan, United Methodist pastor and mentor, whose insights have enriched my writings, especially this one.

Immeasurable thanks and gratitude go to author Michael Hartnett of Long Island, New York and author of *Generation Dementia, Fools in the Magic Kingdom* and more recently, *The Blue Rat*, who read and edited the final draft. Kudos also to Black Rose Writing for publication. Reagan Rothe, owner and publisher of Black Rose Writing, and his staff for their guiding insights, suggestions and title recommendation.

In writing *Torched: Summer of '64*, for history and facts, I relied heavily on the following invaluable resources:

—*The Summer That Didn't End: The Story of the Mississippi Civil Rights Project of 1964* by Len Holt
—*Local People: The Struggle for Civil Rights in Mississippi* by John Dittmer
—*Civil Rights Chronicle: Letters from the South* by Clarice T. Campbell

This novel would never have seen the light of day if one individual had not read the first pages and encouraged me to continue. That was almost thirty years ago. Thank you, Sandi.

ABOUT THE AUTHOR

Joe Edd Morris is the author of the novels *Land Where My Fathers Died*, *The Last Page*, *The Prison* and nonfiction works including *Revival of the Gnostic Heresy: Fundamentalism* and *Ten Things I Wish Jesus Hadn't Said*. His short fiction has appeared in literary journals with a nomination for the Pushcart Prize. Morris is a retired United Methodist minister and psychologist. He and his wife, Sandi, live in Tupelo, MS.

NOTE FROM THE AUTHOR

Word-of-mouth is crucial for any author to succeed. If you enjoyed *Torched: Summer of '64*, please leave a review online—anywhere you are able. Even if it's just a sentence or two. It would make all the difference and would be very much appreciated.

Thanks!
Joe Edd

Thank you so much for reading one of our **Thrillers**.

If you enjoyed our book, please check out our recommended for your next great read!

The Tracker by John Hunt

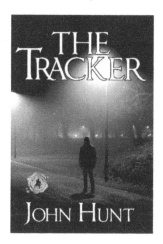

"A dark thriller that draws the reader in." *–Morning Bulletin*

"I never want to hear mention of bolt-cutters, a live rat and a bucket in the same sentence again. EVER." *–Ginger Nuts of Horror*

CPSIA information can be obtained
at www.ICGtesting.com
Printed in the USA
LVHW092109060722
722768LV00014B/421

9 781684 334742